WINNER OF THE COVETED EDGAR AWARD!

THE GREEN STONE

Another top-quality, prize-winning novel of suspense from Lancer!

D0556456

THE
GREEN
STONE

by

SUZANNE BLANC

LANCER BOOKS • NEW YORK

A LANCER BOOK • 1966

THE GREEN STONE

This Lancer edition published by arrangement with
Harper & Row, Publishers, Incorporated.

LANCER BOOKS, INC. • 185 MADISON AVENUE • NEW YORK, N.Y. 10016

THE NEW HIGHWAY from Monterrey to Mexico City sweeps through rocky, barren countryside. It is a fast, lonely road, traveled little by tourists who have time to take the more picturesque coastal route. Here and there are a few clumps of trees that have not yet been cut down for the rude lean-tos of the northern Indian villages. Stretching out on either side are the rolling hills that grow gradually steeper as the road nears San Luis. The landscape subtly changes, growing rockier. The twig villages are replaced by an occasional adobe hut, but most of the villages lie out of sight, just behind the crest of the flanking hills, so that the road seems to race through an empty, untenanted world.

From one of these little villages, just twenty-five miles north of San Luis, three men walked down a rough dirt road to the intersection with the new highway. Their flat, dark faces were shaded by huge, woven hats, their dun-colored clothes merged into the background behind them, the sun glinted on the long barrels of their rifles. They walked single file along the highway until they came to a sharp curve and there they squatted down behind the rocks—talking a little, at first; then silent, half drowsing in the afternoon sun.

When the first, faint throb of a distant motor reached them the older man stood up, reaching for his rifle. He peered out from under his broad-shaded hat, spat on the ground beside the others. "One of the big ones," he said and spat again. They watched silently and unseen as the huge truck, skidding as it took the sharp turn, rumbled by, throwing a shower of small rocks at their hiding place. Twice more they were alerted by the big trucks that roared between the border and Mexico City while the sun moved steadily toward the horizon, and the heat of the day faded.

Finally a car appeared, just a shimmering speck in the distance at first, but even before they could see it clearly, they all stood up, grabbing their rifles. As the car grew larger, the old one grinned. "*Turista*," he said and crouched down again, bracing the barrel of the gun on the high rock in front of him. The others knelt beside him, tense with waiting, but only their eyes showed the tenseness, their eyes and the hands that held the rifles. To the men behind the rocks there seemed to be nothing in the world except them and the road and the approaching car.

In the yellow Cadillac, Mrs. Randall, a plump, rather pretty woman in her late forties, said for the hundredth time, "I don't know why we took this road—there's nothing to see. We might as well have flown down."

Mr. Randall, who secretly liked the fast, empty road, increased his speed and said placatingly, "I know, Clara, but you'll have to admit we made good time. We'll be in San Luis in less than an hour."

It was at that second that the bullet shattered the windshield and struck him in the left eye. The impact turned him around and his hand convulsively gripped the steering wheel so that the car careened across the road, missing the curve and crashing into the rocks, a tangled mass of glass, chrome and metal. It happened so fast that Mrs. Randall had no time even to scream. She was suspended for a second in space, then thrown through the broken windshield and onto the crumpled hood, her pretty, flowered dress stained by the dun-colored dust that mingled with the darkness of her blood.

The Indians scurried from behind the rocks. The older one was saying with satisfaction, "Just like the last time. Remember, nothing but the pesos." His sons looked and nodded with respect.

It was not hard for the father to find the man's wallet stuffed fat with peso notes. His son Carlos saw the expensive camera lying on the floor and reached for it. Manuel, scarcely more than a boy, simply stood in the road staring at the broken body of Mrs. Randall stretched on the hood of the car.

One arm was outstretched at a grotesque, rigid angle and seemed to be pointing at him. On one of the white, plump fingers was a ring, a silvery ring with a translucent green stone. Gingerly Manuel reached out and pulled the ring from her finger, held it for a minute, then slipped it under his belt.

"Hey, Manuel, what you doing?" the old man asked.

"Nothing, Father, just looking."

Just then the old one noticed the camera already slung over Carlos' shoulder. He reached out and cuffed his son viciously across the face. "Put it back," he said. "Remember the last time."

It was not easy to forget the last time. The villagers had heard the crash and had run down the hill to the road to help, but the tourists were already dead. And since the dead cannot use things of this world, the Indians had taken these things and brought them back to the village. The police had come, shouting and asking questions, and had taken everything away, the tires, the horn, the pretty clothes, even things that hadn't belonged to the dead *turistas* the police had taken, everything except the pesos.

Remembering, Manuel wanted to put the ring back,

but the others were watching him, and he was afraid of his father, so he simply fingered the bulge the ring made under his belt and hurried up the hill after them, wishing he had not taken the ring, wondering where he could hide it.

The entire village had heard the crash, but no one had come to the road. Instead they talked about it and wondered if the police would come again to ask questions in harsh voices and to search the huts. "If we do not go to the road," they said, "the police cannot come, because we know nothing, we have taken nothing." The logic seemed so irrefutable that no one worried about the mass of metal and glass that lay just over the crest of the hill.

Only Manuel worried. The ring pressed against the tender skin of his belly like a small, round knot of fear. He would have liked to throw it away, but wherever he looked someone seemed to be watching him. "Later," he decided, "when everyone is asleep, I can go back and put the ring on the señora's hand."

Just at dusk, when the darkness was gathering, a truck driver narrowly missed the wreck. He stopped, saw the man in the car, the body on the hood, both lying in the unnatural stillness of death. Hastily he turned his mammoth freight truck around and roared back to San Luis. By nightfall the first of the police cars arrived with their shrieking sirens. Torches like flickering candles suddenly burned in the immensity of the night. Reflectors on the roadblocks set up at either end of the curve winked with dim, red eyes. Beams crisscrossed the black road like searchlights as the police moved the bodies and measured the skid marks. There was the smashing of glass against the rocks, the clatter of metal, and finally a creaking groan as the broken hulk of the car was hoisted on its rear wheels and hauled away. One by one the lights on the road blinked out, the police sirens rose to a crescendo,

8

diminished and finally faded away, leaving utter silence on the road, the rocks, the hill, the village.

Now Manuel knew it was too late to replace the ring, and he lay on the dirt floor of the hut wrapped in indecision.

"If the police find the ring," he worried, "they will know it belonged to the *turista*. There will be questions, they will shout at me and then they will take the ring away." Everything the police had taken before: things that belonged to the tourists, things that belonged to the village. Only the pesos they hadn't taken. "One peso is like another," the police had said. "Who can tell who owned a peso?"

"One ring is not like another," Manuel reasoned. "But the green stone. One stone is like another, prettier perhaps, but who can tell where it came from?" And so in the darkness of the hut, with his hunting knife, Manuel carefully pushed apart the prongs that held the emerald, and when it was light enough outside for him to see, he climbed over the sleeping bodies of his brother and father, walked to the crest of the hill and threw the setting as far away as he could.

The flat, green stone was in a leather pouch around his neck when he rolled up once again on the floor to sleep. But through the leather the stone seemed still to burn his skin, reminding him that he was guilty, that he had disobeyed his father. It was almost dawn before Manuel fell asleep.

The sun slowly pushed its way over the horizon, casting long golden paths on the hillside. Its rays fell on the setting that had caught on a small scrublike bush and glistened on the diamonds that had surrounded the emerald. Above, a solitary crow saw the sparkling object on the ground, swooped down and carried the shining bauble away.

one

THE PREFECTURE of police in San Luis is on a side street, a large barn of a building that looks and smells like police stations all over the world. Behind it, across a connecting courtyard, are the government offices in what was, at one time, a nunnery. Few recall the religious origin of the building; all religious symbols have been removed, the chapel is now a reception hall, the nuns' cells with their arch-shaped windows are offices for the Federal branches of investigation.

On the night the Randalls were killed, it was to one of these offices, ambiguously marked "Tourist Section," that Sergeant Roberto brought the accident reports. It was late and he had merely intended to place the manila folder on Inspector Menendes' desk and leave for home, but, as usual when he was assigned to work with the inspector, he worried.

The inspector was an educated Indian, a unique product of his generation, difficult to work with, exacting, and, to the sergeant's city-bred mind, incomprehensible. He always wanted information for which there was no allowance on the official forms. He would ask searching questions such as "What was your impression?" or "Did you feel that anything was wrong?" He had been thoroughly trained in established police methods, but often

10

ignored them, relying instead on uncanny, primordial instincts that lay just below his civilized veneer.

Because of the protuberant blue eyes he had inherited from his German mother, Sergeant Roberto was inclined to forget his own Indian heritage. In the conscious reaches of his mind was a contempt for all Indians.

Beneath this, however, was a substratum of awe in relation to the inspector, a vestigial fear of the unknown that could be traced to one of his more distant ancestors, for the sergeant never looked at the massive Indian with his immobile face without being reminded of a grim Aztec idol.

No matter how often the sergeant worked with him, the inspector remained remote and inscrutable. The educated speech, the command of Spanish, English, and French, the phenomenal memory, the machinelike efficiency of the mind assumed the quality of supernormal powers in that huge, primitive body. Beside him the sergeant felt dwarfed and insignificant. He found himself making clumsy mistakes, omitting important facts from his reports or writing them down without noticing their significance.

Now, as he placed the folder on the inspector's desk, a vague unsureness nagged at him as if once again he had overlooked something obvious. The scene on the road came back, eerie in the torchlight, almost a tableau carefully arranged and then left untouched. Just what was wrong eluded him. It was, after all, a dangerous curve and, as in the case of the tourists who had been killed there the month before, the skid marks showed that the driver had been going too fast. Still, there was this nagging dissatisfaction.

"This is what comes of working with that educated savage," he decided in disgust at himself.

However, as though he had no volition of his own, he picked up the folder again and skimmed through its contents. Everything was in order, the detailed description of the accident complete with diagrams and photographs, the report of the other accident that had happened at the same curve, the careful inventory of the tourists' belonging all neatly listed: clothes, entry permit, driver's license, camera, money. . . . It was here the sergeant's eye stopped. Money. Over fifteen hundred dollars was listed in American traveler's checks and twenty-eight dollars in United States currency—yet only a few centavos of change, and those had been found in the woman's purse.

Would rich North Americans be traveling without pesos? Possible, of course, but what if it were found that some money were missing? That would change this from an ordinary accident to robbery, especially if a large sum were involved. As they always were, the police would be held responsible and in this case Sergeant Roberto himself could be suspected. It was an uncomfortable thought. There was, of course, the truck driver, who could have robbed the bodies, but without knowing that money was actually missing was he justified in ordering the driver held for questioning? Best not to take a chance. Roberto picked up the telephone.

"Chiquita," he said to the operator. "Get me the police desk."

Once he had ordered the driver brought in, he could no longer delay notifying the inspector. In the final analysis the case was Menendes' responsibility. He decided to drop in casually at the inspector's apartment and give him a rapid review of the events.

On the way it occurred to him that he had no evidence on which to justify the arrest of the truck driver, that he had acted precipitously, motivated by a self-interest that had no place in police work. He could imagine the inspector contemptuously explaining all this to him, and he almost turned back. But once started, he was under a compulsion to continue. He decided to let fate call the turn. If the inspector's apartment were dark, he would return to the police station and order the driver's release.

The apartment was brightly lighted. Theresa Menendes greeted him warmly at the door. Under a coating of powder her pleasant face was flushed with excitement. Her plump body overflowed in soft white rolls at the square neckline. Over her shoulder the sergeant could see people sitting around the living room awkwardly holding dishes of ice cream.

"I'm sorry, Señora Menendes," the sergeant said. "I didn't know you were having a party."

"It's all right, Sergeant. We're just celebrating María's first communion. Please come in."

"No, thank you. If I could just speak to the inspector for a minute."

To the inspector the sergeant's arrival was a welcome relief. He had not approved of the party from the beginning but had been unable to resist his daughter's pleas or Theresa's tears. Considering himself an emancipated man he disapproved of the church as a form of ignorant superstition fit only for women and children. If his wife and child wished to attend services he had no objection, but he did not want the church brought into his home. He had known that Theresa would invite her relatives and the neighbors in the building. It had not occurred to him that she would include the parish priest: a nice enough little man, but the humble way in which his family addressed him as "Padre" infuriated the inspector. To think that this symbol of mental bondage could exist in the hearts of his wife and daughter annoyed him so much that he sat all evening in a hostile silence that dampened the spirits of his guests. When Theresa told him the sergeant was waiting, he eagerly seized the excuse to get away from the overcrowded room, the guests, the priest, and the ice cream.

The two men went out together onto the patio where it was cool and quiet, pleasant with the fresh, green smell of growing plants and the gentle tinkle of the fountain. They sat on the fountain's raised edge.

In the darkness the sergeant couldn't see the inspector's expression, just his huge silhouette, the round shape of his head.

Dryly, factually he described the accident. "It happened at that bad curve. The car went into a sharp skid and crashed into the rocks. The man must have died instantly, crushed against the steering wheel. . . . The woman probably bled to death."

The inspector stiffened to attention. "And no one helped? What about the Indians, didn't they hear the crash?"

"Not that we know of. We haven't inquired at the village yet, but apparently nothing in the car was missing. If the Indians had found the wreck, you know how they are . . ." He paused, and the words trailed off into embarrassed silence.

"You say apparently nothing is missing, but are you sure? Have you checked with customs to see if the tourists declared anything of value when they entered Mexico?"

"No, it seemed like a simple accident. The skid marks show they were driving too fast." Even to the sergeant the words sounded like a bumbling excuse. He had been smoking too much. His mouth was parched and raw. Now he suddenly wanted another cigarette, lit it, took one deep, scorching drag and flicked it away in a long arc that was a speck of an ember glowing in the dark.

The inspector stood up and began to pace the patio like a huge, restless, two-dimensional shadow. He was talking quietly as if to himself.

"With tourists there are no simple accidents. There

14

will be inquiries. Someone in the States will say that something was stolen. They will imply the police took it. There will be an investigation." He stopped suddenly and asked, "If you thought it was so simple an accident, why did you come here tonight? Couldn't it have waited until morning?"

Embarrassed, the sergeant told him about the money. "It worried me, rich tourists traveling without Mexican pesos."

"It should worry you." The inspector sounded pleased, as if an idiot son had at last learned to tie his own shoe-laces. "I suppose you picked up the truck driver?"

Sergeant Roberto nodded, then, realizing that the inspector could not see his movements in the darkness, said aloud, "Yes, he should be at the station now." He continued apologetically, "It never occurred to me to hold him when he reported the accident. He's a short man, very fat, and he was crying, actually crying, even by the time I got there he was still crying."

"Of course we don't know whether anything's missing," the inspector said. "That's one of the things we'll have to find out. I suppose, however, we'd better talk to him."

At the police station there was only one man on duty. He sat with his feet on the desk reading a movie magazine. Behind him, perched uneasily on a bench, was the driver, a fat, untidy man who apprehensively watched the approach of the big plain-clothes Indian and the police sergeant. At first he was almost incoherent as he tried to describe the wreck, but somehow he conveyed the untouched quality that even the sergeant had noticed. He mentioned the woman's purse lying in the middle of the road.

"I couldn't even touch that," he said. "And as for the *turistas*, I could see that they were dead. It was so quiet there I was afraid to go near the car." The stout man blanched at the memory and automatically crossed himself.

Taking turns the sergeant and the inspector alternately questioned and cross-questioned him, while the other policeman sat withdrawn and indifferent to everything except his magazine.

The driver tried to give details, but his childlike mind seemed to be blocking out the scene. He kept saying over and over again, "It was terrible, Señores, you can't believe how terrible."

Casually the inspector asked him about the money.

The driver looked at him in amazement. "If some money's gone, I didn't take it. I didn't even think about it. I thought only of getting help."

They searched him, found only a few crumpled peso notes. The inspector took his name, address, and released him.

"A man like that," he explained to the sergeant, "is too afraid of the police to lie. If he had taken any money, the last thing he would have done is report the accident."

But Sergeant Roberto was not convinced. "Where is the money, then?"

"We don't even know if any is missing," the inspector reminded him sharply. "Get the police in Monterrey started on that. Have them check all possible places of exchange, the hotels, the banks, the shops. If they find nothing have them contact the police in Nuevo Laredo. While you're doing that I'll wire for the customs declaration."

When the necessary telegrams were sent, it was very late. The reports could not be expected until morning. By the time they finally left the police station, the man at the desk had dropped his magazine on the stone floor and was snoring gently. Outside, in the east, the sky was tinged with a faint, gray light.

16

two

ON THE SAME afternoon the Randalls were killed, Jessie
Prewitt came through the customs at Nuevo Larado. She
was a well-dressed woman in her middle thirties, but because of her small size and the closely cropped brown
hair, at first glance she appeared to be very young. Tiny
lines etched at the corners of her eyes and mouth betrayed her, the lines and the distracted air with which she
signed the thick sheaf of papers and answered what
seemed to be a succession of idle questions. Where was
she going? How long did she plan to stay? How much
money was she bringing in? Did she have a camera, gun,
jewelry, extra tire?

There was advice, too, gratuitous advice about the
highways, hotels, gasoline, all of which she heard faintly
and recorded in the same remote way in which she was
hearing and recording everything these days. The Am-
bassador in Monterrey was very fine, there was a lovely
modern church there, well worth seeing. It was possible
to cut off at San Luis for Morelia, a lovely old colonial
city. Near Morelia they did the butterfly-net fishing,
very interesting, very old. Was the señora traveling alone?
Well, then it would be best to take the new road to Mexico City, not so interesting as the old road, but faster,
shorter, and at San Luis there were fine accommodations,
a church that dated from the eighteenth century.

Only after all the advice had been given did the customs official finally stamp Jessie's papers, seal her luggage and help her back into the car.

It was well past noon. The streets of the sprawling border town were crowded with people, carts, cars, children, dogs. A man with a pile of bright-colored scarves across his arm called to her from the sidewalk, "Very pretty, Señora. Very cheap. You buy!" A dirty little boy ran along beside the car yelling something she couldn't understand. And the annoyance of threading her way through the narrow streets made her wonder, as she had several times during the past few days, why she had taken this trip at all.

When she finally left the outskirts behind her and was actually on the highway, the annoyance faded and Jessie slipped back into the torpor that had followed her on the long drive from California, across Arizona, through Texas. The bleak, hot, colorless landscape rolled past, each endless mile like the last. There was little traffic, her car seemed to drive itself, and Jessie had time to relive again, as she had done mile after mile, the pain of the last week.

"It was so sudden," she thought for the hundredth time. "I wasn't prepared for it." And yet, underneath, she knew that she was prepared, that the disintegration of her marriage had started long before last Sunday. Dan had been drifting away for many months, separated from her by some sort of self-absorption that she couldn't penetrate. There were the long silences, the sudden rages, the fishing and hunting trips she couldn't share. There were the long, awkward evenings filled with trivial chatter like that of two strangers meeting on a plane of casual indifference. There were her own rebellions and resentments that flared into articulate anger only to be followed by days of stiff, awkward civility. And there was the dropping away of their mutual friends whom Dan no longer made an effort to please, and new friends who belonged either to her or to Dan, but not to them as a couple.

"I shouldn't have been surprised. I should have known." Yet how could she really know that fourteen years of marriage had become a cage to Dan? Wasn't that what he had said on Sunday afternoon? Not exactly that. And she forced herself to remember how he looked, what he said. It was so casual, as if he were commenting on the weather.

"You're still young, Jessie, attractive. There's no reason why each of us shouldn't build another life with someone else with whom we can find some happiness."

Then he had poured her a drink and handed it to her, smiling that wide, artificial smile that made everyone think of him as a big, good-natured teddy bear. He continued quietly in the controlled way he always used in talking to her nowadays, "You'll have to admit we have nothing in common."

It was as if he had struck her. She was unable to think . . . even to reply, and he went on as if she had agreed. "We'll split everything down the middle, fifty-fifty. That's fair, isn't it?"

She shook her head silently, still unable to grasp his meaning; and believing she wouldn't accept that settlement, his gray eyes turned agate hard. "Oh, you want it all. Is that it?"

"It isn't the money," Jessie had said. "Only you worry about the money."

"Look, Jess. It can't have been pleasant for you, either. I haven't been nice to you. What do you want me for?"

For a moment she wondered why, and then she answered as honestly as possible. "Habit, I guess."

He started to pace, looking unusually large in the tiny kitchen. "Jessie, I've given you fourteen years of my life. That's enough!"

19

From somewhere inside of her a small core of pride stiffened her to answer. "All right, if that's what you want."

"That's what I want," Dan had said with a finality that allowed no discussion.

At first she couldn't believe it, but later that night the tears came and a terrible feeling of isolation, an urge to run, anywhere, away from herself, from Dan, from the memory of the happy years they had spent together before Dan had changed. Lying awake that night Jessie realized that Dan's words were not unpremeditated; only the timing had not been planned.

Still she hoped he hadn't meant it. In the morning when she came down for breakfast, her face puffed from weeping, conscious of her age, her ugliness, she still hoped that they were idle words impelled by some hidden anger she hadn't recognized.

But she could tell at once she was wrong.

"What are you going to do?" Dan asked.

Again the impulse to run seized her. "I'll go away."

"We're still friends," he said. "Where will you go?"

"I don't know, I'll go away."

Even then she didn't believe it was really happening, that he would leave the house without trying, some way, to change things. But as if it had been a day just like any other day, he finished a second cup of coffee, put on his tweed jacket and left the house and Jessie behind him.

Looking back Jessie could only vaguely remember what she had done that day. At first, frantically, she had started her usual household chores until the futility of them struck her. In the midst of making the bed she had stopped and started to pack. The newspaper boy came and she paid the bill. A sudden dizziness struck her, forcing her to lie down for a few minutes. The telephone started to ring, but by the time she reached it, it had stopped. Then she returned to her packing, driven by a haste she couldn't understand. She fought a terrible impulse to call Dan, to beg him.

At last there was nothing else to do, no excuse to linger, and she piled the bags into her convertible. It seemed to her as she backed out of the driveway that she heard the phone ring again. . . . But now, for some unexplained reason, it seemed too late.

She had thought only of going to a hotel, but when she stopped at the bank for money, she passed a poster advertising Mexico and, with an impulse born partly of the need to run and partly of an unrealized desire to be somewhere very different, she decided that she would go to Mexico.

All that night she drove, and most of the next day, until exhaustion forced her to stop her headlong flight and to sleep. When she awakened she didn't know, at first, where she was, only that something terrible had happened. At the first quickening of memory, she felt again the impulse to run.

Now, four days later, the pain had subsided, and she wondered what she was doing alone in this strange country driving down a road so hot and colorless that there was nothing to distract her from the endless repetition of her memories. But she could not and would not turn back, because the further she drove, the more clear it became that there was nothing to turn back to.

She reached Monterrey in the early afternoon, coming suddenly on a wide boulevard planted with trees, a few houses, then, all at once, streetcars, many buildings, people.

At the hotel there were the usual Americans who had taken the short drive from the border to spend a few inexpensive days in Mexico, yet it was still too close to home for the casual acquaintances that spring up between Americans in foreign lands. Jessie was very much aware of her aloneness.

21

She wandered idly around the streets close to her hotel, and what would have been an exciting experience with Dan was a barren one without him. She kept seeing things that would have interested him . . . a silversmith's shop . . . a sandal store . . . a miniature replica of an ancient Spanish galleon. When she went into the luxurious hotel dining room with its hundreds of caged birds, she kept thinking how much Dan would have enjoyed all this.

After dinner she stopped at the desk, unconsciously seeking the warmth of a human contact. The desk clerk was a friendly, lemon-colored man in a gray, pin-striped suit who spoke English with a soft, liquid accent. Like the customs official he was eager to give her information, talking constantly as he unfolded a large road map.

"The old road to the capital is picturesque, Señora. You go through the jungle." He pointed to a jagged line running along the gulf. "There's a new road, much shorter, very fast." He stopped abruptly and looked at her with large, brown eyes. "If the Señora is driving alone, the new road would probably be better. But you must not drive too fast. Sometimes there are rocks or cattle on the highway. There have been some bad accidents. On the radio tonight I heard that two *turistas* were killed on that highway. Señor and Señora Randall. Very tragic. They were right here at this hotel last night. Did you know them?"

Jessie shook her head.

"Very nice people. Very rich," he said sadly. "You see you must drive slowly, you can't see Mexico if you go too fast."

Remembering the uninteresting landscape from the border to Monterrey, Jessie smiled.

The clerk, thinking the little señora was pleased by his advice, smiled too. "It's easy to find the highway, just two blocks from the hotel. You'll see the big trucks. Follow them west. After a while the road turns off to the south. It's an easy day's drive from here to San Luis."

That night, lying in the strange hotel room, Jessie thought unexpectedly about the couple who had been killed. She wondered how old they were, whether they still cared for each other. "If I had been here yesterday, perhaps I would be the one who was dead." Although the idea had no reality for her, it was, somehow, a comforting one.

Early the next morning before any of the other guests were up, Jessie left Monterrey. Her white convertible followed mile for mile the same road the Randalls had taken toward San Luis.

three

THE EARLY MORNING hours were cool in San Luis; the first sounds of day were brisk, as if the few people on the street and the horses drawing produce-laden carts to market all moved rapidly for warmth.

Inspector Menendes, who had been tossing on the living-room couch, covered himself with an afghan and settled back for another hour of rest. So far his sleep had been punctuated by worry about the accident report that would have to be written. He thought of Mrs. Randall slowly bleeding to death, of the Indians who had not come to help her, of the telegrams sent to the border.

Actually the wires were merely good procedure, and he expected little of importance in the answers. The questions he had asked of the sergeant were the very ones that would be asked of him. Since his subordinate insisted on following exact police procedure, let him at least be thorough. Knowing the sergeant's attitude toward his own unorthodox methods, the inspector took grim pleasure in pointing out Roberto's omissions; yet on the whole he preferred working with Roberto than with any of the other regular police. Honest and painstaking, in time, with the proper guidance, he would make a good detective. Already he was beginning to notice facts that were out of context, like the shortage of pesos. Nevertheless, the inspector knew that unless a huge sum

24

were involved, tracers would be futile. And as for anything else, the untouched quality of the wreck as shown in the photographs indicated that nothing of importance would be missing.

Now, as he closed his eyes again, Menendes thought of the photographs, searching for something that eluded him. Only for a moment he saw them clearly, then yielded to the warmth of the cover and sleep.

The sun was shining brightly when he awakened. The street outside was alive with activity: a strident quarrel between two women, the screams of playing children, the excited barking of dogs, the insistent call of a fruit peddler. Next door the baby was crying for attention. His own apartment lay in silence.

María must already have left for school. Theresa, he knew, would be in the bedroom, waiting for him to apologize for his behavior at the party. If he went in there she would greet him with tearful reproaches and after a long, emotional outburst would forgive him. Usually he accepted his role in these scenes which were the meat of Theresa's existence, but, today, occupied by the unpleasant prospect of writing the report on the tourists' accident, he left the house without even seeing her.

At the office there was a telegram waiting for him from the border, but because he expected so little from it, it was with no sense of immediacy that he opened it. At first he couldn't believe what he read. The Randalls had declared two items—a German camera worth four hundred dollars and an emerald ring valued at twelve thousand dollars. Automatically the inspector pulled out the inventory of the tourists' possessions. The camera was listed. The ring was missing.

Had anyone except Sergeant Roberto been in charge at the accident, the inspector would have suspected the police. The inspector sat in uncomfortable silence anticipating the inevitable session with the Department of

Tourism; then, without transition, he remembered the photographs and his intention of re-examining them.

Stark, clear, with every detail magnified, the one he was looking for showed the soft shoulder of the road, the boulders and the front end of the car. In the sand near the boulders were shallow indentations that could have been footprints—at least the inspector imagined that he saw the imprint of a rope-soled sandal. Perhaps because he could not accept the complete absence of the Indians, the impression was woven purely of the fabric of his own mind, but stubbornly he clung to it.

Admittedly the marks were a slender thread on which to build a case. Nevertheless it was the only one he had, and it must be followed if for no other reason than his report to Mexico City could include it. He picked up the telephone and asked for Sergeant Roberto.

The sergeant, handsome in his tailor-made black uniform, looked rested and cheerful. Because of his belief in the inspector's supernormal powers, the customs report came as no surprise to him. Perversely this annoyed the inspector, and when the sergeant asked, "Shall I pick up that driver again?" the inspector snapped "No! I told you last night the man knows nothing. Another driver perhaps—this one, no."

Sergeant Roberto stood at attention as the inspector continued.

"You will take two men and an interpreter, go to the Indian village, question everyone and tear that place apart for the ring. Dig up the floors of the huts, check the eaves, search the Indians. Something tells me that ring is in the village, and I want the place turned inside out to find it."

"What about the money?"

"There is still no evidence that any is missing. We are probably exceeding our authority in making even this search. I will assume the responsibility for that; however,

I am holding you responsible for the behavior of the men you select. No matter what you find, I want nothing touched except the ring. Is that clear? Well, what are you waiting for?"

"Inspector, if the Indians were at the wreck, surely they wouldn't have taken only the ring and the money. You know how it usually is. Last time they stole everything, even parts of the car."

Inspector Menendes nodded and pursed his large lips thoughtfully. "If the entire village were there that would be true. The untrammeled appearance of the scene indicates that for some unknown reason the village did not rush to the road. However, let us assume that one Indian, or perhaps two were there. What would they take? Anyway, now that we know that such a valuable ring is gone, we can't afford to overlook the possibility that it is in the village."

When the inspector was alone again, he started the distasteful task of writing his preliminary report. It was one thing to give an accounting of a case that was neatly completed, but at this stage when there were so many intangibles and no progress, any report would make him appear inadequate. The missing ring certainly complicated what would be otherwise a routine matter. Perhaps Sergeant Roberto would find it at the village. In any case, a few hours of delay could make little difference in the capital. The inspector put aside the blank sheet of paper and looked through his mail.

There was a bulky letter from the Ortega mortuary. That would contain the forms to fill out for shipment of the bodies, but since the inspector did not yet have the necessary information from the United States consul, he put that one aside. There was a complaint forwarded from the Department of Tourism that one of the smaller San Luis hotels was not charging the posted rates. This would require a routine investigation and report. There was a request from the University to lecture on criminal psychology, leaving a date open that would be convenient for him. He answered that letter, clipped the "Please show cause" form to the hotel complaint, addressed and stamped them both and put them into the out-basket.

Now, since there was nothing left to do, he opened the letter from the mortuary. Inside were the necessary shipment papers, but attached to them were two notes, one typed, the other scribbled in a spidery, almost illegible hand.

Even before he read them Inspector Menendes knew that something was very wrong, and when he finished, his heart was pumping wildly. The letter clearly stated that Mr. Randall had died not as the result of the accident, but from a high-velocity rifle bullet that had entered his eye, passed through his brain and left a large hole in the back of his skull. The mortician had concluded with polite inquiries about the inspector's health and the destination of the bodies. The handwritten note was from a Dr. Espinosa whom the mortician had called, and it verified the information in more technical detail.

For a few seconds the inspector felt that he had lost his bearings. The office was suddenly oppressively hot and unfamiliar. Although he understood the words in the letter, at first he couldn't grasp that an ordinary accident case had turned into murder. Once he accepted the idea, however, the solution of the crime appeared relatively uncomplicated. The missing money, the ring, were leads to the murderer, and he was convinced they would be found in the village. Only an Indian could have planned a crime with such simplicity.

He picked up the phone and asked for the commandant of police, and received the assurance that the bullet would be found, either at the scene of the crime or in the wreckage of the car, and brought to him. "The machinery of the law is at your command, Inspector," the pompous voice at the other end of the line assured him, but behind the bland assurance was the definite impression that, though the police would co-operate, the responsibility of solving the murder of the tourists remained his.

Actually he was confident that within a few hours he would be able to arrest the criminal. The bullet would be another link in the chain of evidence against him. He wired a long, optimistic report to the capital and settled back to wait.

Time seemed to pass very slowly. By two o'clock he was hungry and impatient, but since he didn't want to leave the office, he had some cold and tasteless food sent in from a nearby café.

Shortly before three o'clock a policeman brought him two white envelopes containing the bullets. One had been found on the road, apparently shattered by the rocks. The other, taken from the wreckage of the car, was also damaged and, as evidence, equally useless.

The bullets were thirty-thirty's, confirming the mortician's conclusion that Mr. Randall had been killed by a high-velocity rifle—probably, the inspector decided, a Winchester. It was not uncommon for the villagers to have modern rifles. It had been many years since they had used old Spanish guns and fowling pieces. Collectors had scoured the villages offering fabulous prices for antiques, and the Indians had gladly replaced them with more efficient, modern weapons. After examining the bullets, the inspector no longer doubted that the crime had been committed by an Indian from the nearby village. But which Indian? The bullets couldn't tell him. His only hope of finding the murderer lay in Sergeant Roberto's return with the ring.

four

LUIS PÉREZ was a familiar figure in the Indian village. At least once each week he brought a group of tourists from San Luis to watch the pottery making. The women were generally the ones who wanted to go to the village, yet once they were there they would walk hesitantly down the center of the road looking at the Indians with uneasy eyes. The men were less cautious. They carried supplies of candy or chewing gum in their expensive, well-cut jackets, and the children had learned to cluster around them shyly waiting for sweets. The tourists, impressed by the continuity of the centuries, always bought pieces of pottery, marveling over the primitive methods of producing it and the ancient designs.

To the Indians the tourists had become part of the economic fabric of their communal life. Almost at a glance they could judge, from the size of the cars in which the visitors arrived, from the quality of their clothes, how much the visitors would spend.

To Luis, the tours had long ago become monotonously boring. The crude huts, the piles of refuse, the heat of the kilns, the oppressive odors had ceased to be picturesque. He saw only the dirt, the poverty, the ignorance and the greed of the Indians.

Now, as he thought of the trip ahead, of the *turistas* waiting for him at the Plaza Hotel, it was with distaste.

He was late. He would have to hurry. Automatically he brushed his camel's-hair coat and stuffed the pockets with tobacco pouches filled with semiprecious stones wrapped in tissue paper. Often he could sell a few of these to the lady tourists. At least, he admitted to himself, the morning was cool; but even the inviting freshness of the day did not mitigate the unpleasant prospect of catering to the foreigners. Each succeeding hour was one in an endless chain of waiting for the startling changes that had been predicted in his future.

The waiting had begun several months earlier when he consulted a fortuneteller. She was famous in the district, an old woman, almost blind, who, it was said, retained the knowledge of the ancient ones and was consulted by the most prominent officials. According to rumor she could even foretell the numbers on the National Lottery, but this seemed incredible to Luis as she was very poor. But whether that was true or not, her powers were eerie. In prophesying his future she had used not only the date of his birth, the position of the stars, but magic, too—a great, flat bowl of sand into which she had blown until the white grains piled in ridges and hollows that represented, she said, his world.

Just thinking of the woman, her seamed, brown skin, milky eyes, the cadence of her flat, ominous voice, a tingle of awe ran like an icy hand along the nape of Luis' neck. First she had traced his past. "Far to the north you were born," she said. "And you lived in a strange land where a harsh language is spoken. Until recently you were very poor."

It was all true. Luis had been born close to the Texas border. His father had crossed the Rio Grande to work in the California vineyards when Luis was still very small. There they had lived in a one-room shack with a cement floor that was cold and damp during the winter. With the children of other migrant workers Luis went to school. He learned English, history, the names of movie stars, a colorful and profane vocabulary and all about the American way of life. At fourteen he stole a car, and, as a result, his family was deported along with hundreds of other illegal immigrants. His father then opened a small leather shop with his meager savings. The family continued to be as poor as ever.

Only after Luis became a guide did he enjoy the creature comforts that others take for granted. He had chosen San Luis as his base of operations both because there were no other guides here and because the city carried his saint's name. He had created his own job, paid heavily for his license and relied on his ingenuity to earn a living from the tourists. Besides conducting tours to the Indian village and around San Luis, there were commissions to be collected from the shops and hotels. There were sometimes lavish tips from the richer tourists.

He was popular with the ladies. Handsome in a sleek, dark fashion, with regular features and a sharp, white smile, he cultivated ingratiating manners that the women found continental and charming. One fatuous elderly woman had given him a gold wristwatch. His expensive coat had been thrown to him in disgust by a businessman whose wife complained that it looked too warm for the Mexican climate.

The coat was Luis' proudest possession: lightweight, belted and with broad, padded shoulders. In it he felt very prosperous, very handsome.

Luis had not done badly from the tourists. He lived in a huge, airy room leading onto a courtyard. He ate well, dressed well and almost always had a few pesos extra. At first just having a room of his own seemed like opulence; then he had discovered the joys of fine clothes, the admiration of women. In contrast with everything he had known in the past, Luis was very rich indeed, and he had been well pleased with himself and his lot until he had consulted the fortuneteller. But once the seeds of discontent were planted, Luis forgot the past and thought only of the future.

Perhaps it is not prophecy at all but the belief in prophecy that fulfills it, for the words of the Indian woman stirred strange chords of impatience in the guide. "There will come a day of great portent," she had intoned, swaying over the sand like a mesmerized cobra. "Unexpected riches and a woman, both from a great distance, mark the beginning of a new path. More I cannot see, for there are many paths for each man, and women and riches can lead him down any one of them."

Riches and a woman from a great distance. What could it mean except that Luis would marry one of the long, silken women from the States to whom a peso was of as little value as a blade of grass? Now he waited impatiently for the day to come. Each time he had an unexpected call from the hotel or the Villa to guide a group of tourists, he studied the faces of the women, wondering, "Is this the one?"

Today he knew she would not be there. He had talked the evening before to the middle-aged women who were waiting for him. They were all inexpensively dressed and equally unprepossessing. The thin one with the wispy gray hair and rimless glasses had introduced herself as "Mrs. Johnson"; her friends, she said, were "Mrs. Mays" and "Mrs. Crane." They had been discouraged by the price of the full-day tour and had compromised on the shorter one just to the Indian village.

It turned out to be an uncomfortable morning. The women's car, no longer new, puffed and groaned over the unpaved road into the hills. The coolness dissipated in hot clouds of dust. The sweat trickled down Luis' back under the warm coat he would not take off. Mrs. Johnson asked endless questions, perhaps because, having paid for his time, she was determined not to waste a moment of it.

And at the village, the Indians were sullen. Here was no rich group of tourists who would buy their pottery. As if the guide and his group were not even there, the Indian women continued to knead the clay, like huge clumps of unleavened bread, roll it and shape it into the pots and dishes that were used everywhere in the area. Even the children seemed to sense that this time there would be no candy or chewing gum, and they stayed close to their mothers, whisking away the flies with withered palm fronds. Here a dog lay panting breathlessly in the road; there a man dozed under the shade of a voluminous hat although it was not yet noon. Near the crude hive-shaped kilns where they baked the pottery even the Indian women suffered from the heat. Their brown faces glistened with beads of sweat. Their white blouses clung to their backs in damp, dark patches.

To Luis in his handsome coat, the temperature was unbearable. He dropped away from the group to pause in the cool shade between two huts and to light a cigarette. It was then that the Indian boy approached him.

The lad was tall, with the well-knit, muscular body of his race. At first glance he appeared to be a man, but the soft layer of fat that still padded his face and the unmasked, vulnerable eyes showed that he was little more than a boy.

"Señor," he said timidly, "I have something to show you." He reached under his shirt for a leather pouch that hung with some religious medals against his coffee-colored, hairless chest and brought out a square-cut stone. Green, almost the color of a lime, its lights shone like those imprisoned in an ice cube. "Very pretty," the boy said. "Very valuable."

At once Luis realized that this was not a worthless gem

like those he sold to the tourists, but of its actual value he had no idea.

"Where did you get it?" he asked sharply.

There was a flicker of expression, almost of fear. "From a *turista*. My father doesn't know."

Could it really be that a tourist, drawn to this dark, dirty boy, had given him the jewel? That didn't seem possible; still, the *turistas* were an unpredictable lot. . . . Or did the boy steal it?

"I'll give you fifty pesos," Luis said doubtfully.

"No, Señor, no. It's very valuable, worth maybe three hundred pesos."

Luis shook his head. "It is a stone, just like any other stone."

The boy became excited. "Señor, it was in a beautiful ring that shone like silver. It belonged to a very rich *norteamericana*."

"Where is the rest of the ring?"

"I threw it away. My father, he didn't want me to have it."

Luis shrugged. "One hundred pesos, no more. Perhaps it is worth nothing. Perhaps I cannot even sell it."

"One hundred pesos, then," the boy said eagerly, handing over the jewel as if it were burning him. "But it's a pretty stone, worth much more."

Luis wrapped the emerald in tissue paper and put it in one of the tobacco pouches beneath some amethysts. Carelessly he dropped the pouch back into his pocket and paid the boy his hundred pesos.

By now his group was ready to leave. Mrs. Crane had bought a piece of pottery, a flat, brown platter with a crude design in tan and green. The woman who sold it was smiling so broadly as she made change that Luis could tell she had charged too much. Several other Indian women had gathered around trying to sell the tourists something else: a potter's mistake that looked like a free-form ash tray, a pitcher shaped like a duck. Walking down the dirt street to the car, the foreigners led a small parade: women carrying pots and bowls, the children dragging palm fronds through the dust, the dogs tagging lazily at the outskirts. The tourists looked straight ahead, talking loudly among themselves as if they didn't see the Indians who followed them.

A dust cloud growling up the hills turned out to be a large sedan. Just as it reached the crest, as though a signal had been given, the Indians scattered to their huts like alarmed chickens. Luis shared their alarm when he recognized a police car.

Ever since he could remember Luis had feared the police. Perhaps the roots of his fear stretched back to the day his father crossed the Rio Grande to work in California, perhaps it dated only from the car theft which had forced them to cross back again. Whatever its origin, whenever a policeman approached him, Luis experienced the same physical uneasiness. Now it took him a conscious effort to smile and nod in a friendly manner to the officers as he helped the women into their car. For their part, the police in their trim black uniforms were extravagantly courteous to the tourists, clicking their heels and saluting smartly while Luis started the motor.

"What was that all about?" Luis wondered aloud, his hand unconsciously searching his pocket to finger the bag of stones.

"We could ask them," one of the women suggested.

"Señora, in Mexico the police ask you; you don't ask them." And with that Luis drove down the hill away from the village.

Somehow he was certain the police were there because of the jewel. That meant it must be very valuable, worth ten times what he had paid for it, a thousand pesos, maybe even more. If he took his time, waited to sell it, he could probably get a good price. He would have liked to examine it again, see it sparkle in the sunshine, reassure himself that it was not merely a piece of glass. One hundred pesos, eight dollars in United States money, that was quite a bit to pay for a piece of glass. No, it was valuable all right. The green stone must have been stolen. Otherwise why would the boy be too frightened to keep it? Why were the police here?

Driving back, Luis thought about the jewel; and the more he thought of it, the more valuable he believed it to be and the more certain he was that it must be stolen. He decided to hold it for a few days. When the police were no longer looking for it maybe he could sell it for enough to buy a car, an old one, of course, but he would paint it black with red wheels. The leather store could make him a fine set of seat covers. . . . Even if it were old it would be a handsome car.

Just before they reached the Plaza in the center of San Luis, they were stopped by a cart that had overturned in the narrow cobblestoned street, spilling a lod of hay. The hay looked dingy as the driver loaded great armfuls back into the cart. They were held up again at the church where a special High Mass had just ended; the old-fashioned women in their black dresses and shawls crowded out onto the Plaza, silently, like penitents. Still, in spite of the delays, they were less than an hour late returning to the hotel.

Because his trip with them had brought him luck, Luis did not charge the women for the extra time. Instead, he displayed his most gracious continental manner, bowing over their withered hands and wishing them *"Buen viaje."*

five

It was the middle of the afternoon before Sergeant Roberto returned from the village. He was in an ugly mood. Dust clung to his immaculate uniform, his hair, his mustache; it coated his boots; its taste, like the unpleasant smell of the Indian huts, lingered in his mouth. The only satisfaction the sergeant could glean from his fruitless afternoon was that the inspector had proved to be wrong. For no reason at all the inspector was suddenly convinced that the Indians were involved in the robbery. It had been a hot, dirty, useless job searching the village, and the truck driver, who, in spite of all of his tears, had probably stolen the ring, was undoubtedly far away by now. Well, it was the inspector who had released him. He'd have to assume the responsibility. If Sergeant Roberto had his way, he'd pick up the man immediately and beat the truth out of him.

The inspector was still sitting behind his desk, just as massive and ugly as when the sergeant had left. At his first sight of Menendes, the sergeant was again struck with his resemblance to one of the granite idols with sightless, obsidian eyes that the Indians still secretly worship.

The inspector was twirling a yellow pencil between his thumb and forefinger. As usual, he let the sergeant stand for several uncomfortable, silent minutes; then, as if it were the subordinate who had kept him waiting, he looked up from the pencil and snapped, "Well, did you find the ring?"

"We found nothing." The sergeant couldn't keep the smug undertones from his voice. "Just the usual silver jewelry and money. The money, of course, could belong to the North Americans, but you told us not to touch it." He shrugged. "Anyway, who can tell one peso from another?"

Inspector Menendes seemed not to notice the critical tone. "You searched everywhere?"

"Everywhere!"

"How did the villagers react? Did they know anything?"

"Who can tell about an Indian? They didn't like having the floors dug up, and a few were angry when we searched them. One man even threatened to tell the government. Where do they get these ideas? Mostly they were just sullen."

The inspector stared at him coldly. "Has anyone left the village since last night?"

"No, all heads were there, two hundred fifteen of them. We searched even the babies."

"Did anyone come to the village?"

"Only the guide with some *turistas*. They bought a pot."

The inspector stood up suddenly, his voice a bellow of irritation. "Don't make me pull this out of you question by question. Was there anything else?"

"No, the Indians did not even hear the crash. You want the ring? I say arrest the truck driver."

"Sit down, Sergeant. No need to stand." The inspector's voice was patient, as though he were dealing with a fractious child. He pointed to a scarred, varnished chair next to the desk. "Sergeant, I have a report here that may make you realize that the truck driver was not involved. It says that the North Americans were killed, not by accident . . . but murdered! There was a hole in the man's head that could have been made only by a rifle bullet. Did the truck driver have a rifle?"

"No."

"Do the Indians own rifles?"

"Many of them."

"It's as simple as that."

Sergeant Roberto asked meekly, "Shall I send someone to find the bullet?"

"It's been done. Two bullets were found, one was smashed against a rock, practically pulverized. The other is equally useless. No rifle marks. They're no good at all to us."

The inspector relapsed into brooding silence. Right now he was distrusting his methods, wondering whether he was indeed clinging too stubbornly to a preconceived idea, but that was impossible. Everything about this crime had an Indian texture. Still, there was something wrong. He had been certain the ring would be found in the village, and it was not there. He projected his mind back to his own youth in his own primitive community before he knew the ways of the outside world. He tried to invoke the simple patterns he had once had as a part of that society. There were facts here that disturbed him, that were at variance with those patterns.

"You say, Sergeant, that the Indians claim not to have heard the crash. . . . Yet, have you ever heard of an accident on our roads when the Indians did not rush out of the villages to enjoy the excitement—sometimes even from miles away?"

The sergeant shook his head. "It does seem odd—but they claim, all of them, to have heard nothing. Could they all be lying?"

"No, that's what's strange. They wouldn't all lie unless it was to protect the community." The words came out unbidden from knowledge long buried in his subconscious and with them the image of a face, round, with tiny, evil eyes almost buried by flesh and a large, loose mouth. It had been so many years since he had thought of the bandit chief that the face at first had meaning for him only as a vague childhood threat. Then the rest of the memory followed. The uncouth band of men who camped in the forest near their village, stealing food from the Indians, sleeping on the ground wrapped in serapes. The frightened village women. The half-understood talk of his elders that to mention the bandits was dangerous. The weeks of living under the shadow of these depraved men. Then the day the soldiers came with questions and promises of protection. How even he, a child of less than eight, had stared blankly at the questions of the soldiers, sharing with the rest of his community a trust in the threats of the bandits—a distrust in the promises of the soldiers. The soldiers left and eventually, too, the robbers vanished, leaving only a small pocket in the collective mind of the Indians.

In their own way, the people are always logical in their simple thinking, Inspector Menendes decided. "There's a reason the villagers did not go to this wreck and one of the Indians knew they would not go," he said aloud.

Sergeant Roberto, uncomfortable, shifted in his chair. "The Chief, the one who was going to report us to the government, said that the police were always the same. He called us robbers."

"That's it!" Inspector Menendes pounded the desk with his massive fist. "What fools we've been." He started rummaging through the papers on the desk. "Here it is, the report on the other accident, the one a month ago at the same spot. 'The car was found stripped, even the tires had been taken. Parts of the car, luggage, a camera, an English book were later recovered from the village.' And this, a complaint registered by the circuit teacher, 'The

Indians claim that the police had taken even things that did not belong to the dead tourists.' Did you check into this, Sergeant?"

"Yes, there was nothing on the inventory to substantiate the complaint."

Inspector Menendes nodded, pursing his lips. "There wouldn't be. But still, it must be true."

"You mean the Indians heard the crash and would not go to the road?"

"It's the only answer. Experience taught them to fear the police. Villages behave this way, in unison, without discussion, simply for social protection."

He picked up the yellow pencil and started twirling it again, his eyes following the revolving planes as if that were all he could see. He was so still that the hot, airless room seemed almost empty except for the loud ticking of the wall clock and the buzzing of a fly beating itself against the dirty window. Sergeant Roberto shifted again, and the wooden chair creaked with his weight. "But you claim an Indian killed those tourists," he said weakly.

The inspector nodded. "Yes, someone from the village who knew the others wouldn't come to the road. He must have fired the shot, taken the money and the ring . . . unless," he added, "by a remote series of coincidences, a stranger, traveling by foot, carrying a rifle could have been on that highway and escaped unseen by anyone." He commented dryly, "My simple Indian mind cannot accept the possibility of such coincidences."

Sergeant Roberto's chair creaked again. "But we didn't find the ring."

"It could be buried outside the village, under a flat stone, in the hollow of a tree, somewhere in the ground. In that case, as soon as the murderer is certain the police will not return, he will dig it up, start wearing it, or bury it with his other treasures in the floor of his hut. We will wait for three or four days, then try again."

As the inspector talked, Sergeant Roberto had been growing increasingly restive, enmeshed by the chain of logic; yet he rebelled against the inactivity it imposed. "And, in the meantime we're just to sit here?"

"In the meantime the tourist bureau in Mexico City will be calling me, demanding action, threatening my job. So in the meantime we do not just sit here."

Menendes outlined then what steps were to be taken. In case the ring had already been sold, pawnshops, jewelry stores, known fences were to be warned. "Tell them that possession of the ring will involve them in a murder case," the inspector said. "Check on anyone who might have been near the village yesterday or today, drivers of the motor freight companies, the tourists who were there this morning. And you might start by bringing in the guide."

It was a relief to the sergeant to leave the office and start some concrete action, to return to the dictates of his own personality. Even if it were fruitless, it was better to be doing something than just to sit patiently until the criminal carelessly exposed himself. The inspector reminded him of a frog, motionlessly watching the movements of a particular fly, certain that if he waited still enough, long enough, the fly would approach.

But the frog in his turn is prey to the hawk. When the telephone rang, the inspector squirmed uneasily at the pleasant feminine voice that said, "Just a moment, Inspector, this is the Department of Tourism calling, go ahead, please, Mexico City."

six

FOR THE LAST several miles the gas indicator on Jessie's convertible had been fluctuating just above zero. The top was down, and the great open expanse of sky above combined with the rocky mesquite-covered landscape to emphasize the emptiness of the barren, desolate road. Occasionally Jessie would pass an Indian, or a group of Indians leading a burro, both men and beasts heavily laden with bulging sacks, primitive, reminiscent of murals by Rivera. Now the diminishing gas in her tank reminded her that she was miles from civilization.

Her eyes, already strained from sleepless nights, burned in the glare of sunshine on the parched earth. Instinctively, to get somewhere, anywhere, quickly, Jessie pressed her foot on the accelerator. The wind through her hair and the monotony of the road lulled her into a type of somnolence, and again she found herself probing her pain as if it were a sore tooth.

Somewhere along the line Dan had changed; just when she couldn't decide. When had he stopped thinking in terms of her? When had he started thinking only of himself?

On the road ahead two vultures hunched over the remains of a small animal. As her car approached they rose on graceful, agile wings to wait for her passing. The vultures, the dead animal, reminded her of BeeBee. They had named him BeeBee because he was so big and black, a wonderful lovable Labrador with tender, dark brown eyes. Dan was out of town when BeeBee disappeared. The dog was often gone for long periods, but this time he didn't return. It took her several days to learn that the Labrador had been shot chasing sheep on a nearby ranch. Jessie had felt an acute sense of loss combined with the worry that BeeBee might have suffered. . . . But more terrible was a formless apprehension of telling Dan. She had always thought of Dan as a gentle man, but all at once she was aware of a violence in him that lay just beneath the surface, a violence that she had refused to recognize. She realized that she could no longer predict his behavior. She had fearful images of his shooting the farmer, and so when he returned she lied to him, telling him that BeeBee had been killed in a road accident. It was the first time Jessie had ever lied to Dan, and for many months it had troubled her.

She tried to trace their separation from each other back beyond that time, but although she knew it had started long before, she was unable to find its origin.

After BeeBee's death she was less free in their relationship, careful not to antagonize Dan so that that, too, became a habit of which she was not consciously aware. Persistently she had refused to see the gulf that lay between them.

Somewhere she had read that if you imagined your worries to be a length of yarn and rolled them into a ball which you then threw away, you would be free of them. But her mind kept groping for the beginning of the yarn without finding it, and the odd sensation of not understanding, of being in a situation without reality continued.

Deliberately she tried to push her mind back to her

childhood, to the time she hadn't known Dan, but even her high-school memories were filled with him. He had moved into the house next door. He had carried her books, taken her to her first prom, bought her the first corsage, tiny red roses framed by a feathery, delicate fern. Remembering how young and vulnerable he was in those days was even more painful than thinking of him as he was now.

She tried to plan ahead to a future without him. It was like learning to walk, facing the unknown without hand-holds or footholds, and Jessie was not yet able to accept a world in which she would have to stand alone.

And so she concentrated on the asphalt road, trying to think only of the miles that passed and those that lay ahead, measuring them against her dwindling supply of gas and her small supply of courage.

A scattering of adobe huts now edged the roadway. There was more traffic, people walking, riding burros, bicycles, carts, automobiles. She rounded a bend and abruptly, without transition, was in the outskirts of San Luis. Ahead was a Pemex station, brilliant white stucco in the sunshine with the familiar white-and-green pumps in front of it.

Small boys clambered over her car when she drew up to the pump, each with a dirty rag with which he inef-fectually dabbed at her windshield. The attendant, tall and thin in a dirty coverall, started to pump gas into her car. She was wondering how to ask him to check the oil when a young man in a handsome, light-tan coat came out of the office and approached the car.

"Welcome to San Luis, Señora," he said in perfect English that was tinged only by a slight, almost indiscernible, intonation. "Permit me to introduce myself. I'm San Luis' official guide."

"Thank you. Could you have the man check my oil?"

The barrage of Spanish that followed seemed quite out of proportion to the simple request, but after many questions, the attendant apparently understood, for he raised the hood of her car.

"I need a hotel, too," Jessie said.

"There's a beautiful one with famous gardens," the guide said. "Run by a North American woman. I've been told the food is excellent. You go to the main street, just this side of the square, turn right and follow the road out over the hill. The Villa Serena is on the right. You'll see the sign."

The attendant who had added oil to her car had now gone after change. A group of tourists in a blue Buick were at the other pump. Behind her a large black car pulled up with a single man at the wheel.

Abruptly the guide leaned toward her. In one hand he was holding a tobacco pouch, in the other a small heap of amethysts nestling against white tissue paper. "These are very nice, Señora," he said urgently. "One hundred pesos, only."

He was so close that Jessie could see a wet film on his forehead and she wondered why he was wearing the warm coat. She didn't want the stones, but she was eager to get away. The attendant had returned with her change. The little boys were holding out sticky hands, clamoring for pesos. In her rear-view mirror she saw the man behind her impatiently open the car door and noticed that he was wearing a black uniform.

The guide was persistent. "Just fifty pesos, Señora. For you fifty pesos," and still leaning toward her, he poured the stones back into the pouch and tossed them into her pocketbook. More because she did not know how to refuse him than for any other reason, Jessie gave him the money.

Again he repeated the directions to the hotel, talking

loudly and gesturing with his arms as if to impress them on her. "Tell them I sent you, Señora, and if you need a guide ask for Luis Pérez."

As she pulled out he was still standing near the pumps watching her, and when she looked back he waved with a broad, friendly grin.

seven

THE GAS STATION served as Luis' business office. By paying a few pesos to the manager he was allowed to wait there for tourists. Usually in the late afternoon hours when the traffic was heaviest, Luis could pick up a few hotel commissions, or arrange a tour; often he could sell a bag of stones.

The only commission he made that afternoon, however, was from a woman traveling alone in a white convertible. She was a tiny woman, pretty in the delicate, colorless way of many North Americans, with light-brown hair and eyes that were as blue and clear as fine aquamarines. At first he had thought she was very young, but then, when he looked more closely, he noticed the tired expression, the small feathery lines near mouth and eyes that come only with age.

It was while he was directing her to the Villa Serena that the police car drew up directly behind them. Sitting at the wheel was the sergeant of police who had been at the village this morning.

The presence of the police, which always evoked vague fears and guilts in him, this time represented present, immediate danger. Convinced that they were searching for the stone, its presence in his pocket urged him to panic. Only long conditioning kept him from running. He knew that he must get rid of the gem quickly and could see only one safe way to do it.

There were doubt and disinterest in the tourist's face as she looked at the amethysts. Perspiration started on his forehead, in the palms of his hands. He could hear, without being able to control it, the unnatural urgency in his voice. Through the rear-view mirror he watched the policeman impatiently open the car door. For a long moment he thought she wasn't going to buy the stones, then reluctantly she handed him fifty pesos. His relief was immeasurable as he tucked the amethysts back over the emerald, drew the strings of the tobacco pouch and tossed it casually into her handbag. Almost immediately his relief mingled with regret at the loss of his treasure. He hoped he had not acted precipitously, but as the sergeant approached him, the regrets evaporated, leaving only relief.

The sergeant nodded in the direction of the departing car. "What did she want?" he asked.

"A hotel. I recommended the Villa Serena."

"But she paid you."

"A tip, the tourists are generous."

Sergeant Roberto raised his eyebrows as though in perplexed admiration at the easy way the guide made his money. "Inspector Menendes would like to see you."

"Why me?" Luis asked. "I've done nothing."

"Something about your license, I think," Sergeant Roberto said vaguely. "You'll have to speak to him."

As the police car wound through the narrow streets of the town, Luis kept thinking of his lost jewel. He hoped he hadn't needlessly discarded it, but he did feel safer without it in his pocket. He forced himself to talk lightly about his work, his success with the ladies, but underneath his uneasiness remained.

They parked not in front of the regular police station but on a side street behind it near the long, low building that had at one time been a nunnery. They followed the stone corridor around a flowerless, tile courtyard with an ugly statue of a cherub holding an urn in the center. Once, water must have fallen from the urn into a drain below, but now the fountain was dry. At the far side of the courtyard they stopped at a door marked TOURIST SECTION.

Inside, the room was little more than a cubicle with scarcely space for a large desk and a few chairs. The man behind the desk was mountainous with a broad, flat face that might have been copied from one of the ancient carvings. His brown suit, tight across the shoulders and chest, exactly matched the color of his skin. On the desk was a small sign with gold letters which read: IN-SPECTOR MENENDES. After the first impact of the man's appearance, Luis' spirits began to rise. He'd had much experience dealing with the Indians and thought little of their intelligence.

The inspector nodded casually toward one of the scarred, empty chairs. The sergeant remained standing at rigid attention near the door as if he were guarding it. There was a long silence, then the inspector folded his hands and asked:

"You were at the Indian village this morning?"

Luis' body tensed. Elaborately he lit a cigarette. "Yes, with some tourists."

"Did you see or hear anything unusual?"

"No, nothing except the police."

"What about the police?"

"They came just as we were leaving. All the Indians ran."

The inspector glared at the sergeant with hard, meaningful eyes, then turned back politely to Luis. "May I see your identification card, please?"

Luis took the white card out of his wallet and handed it to the inspector, who examined it and then started tap-

51

ping it softly on the desk. "In order to deal with tourists as a representative of the Mexican government, a guide must be above reproach. You will not object, therefore, if Sergeant Roberto searches you."

The implied threat that refusal would mean the loss of his license was so obvious that Luis dared not protest. It was comforting to know that the jewel was no longer in his pocket, and he congratulated himself on his cleverness in passing it to the *turista*.

"Of course, Inspector, if it will help in any way."

Sergeant Roberto was thorough. When he found the remaining bags of stones, he emptied them eagerly.

"Just some trinkets I sell to the tourists," Luis explained.

Throughout the proceedings the inspector made no comment. He looked over Luis' belongings, slipped the license into the wallet and handed it back. "I'm sorry we found this necessary. You must understand that we are faced with a serious problem. A very valuable emerald ring was stolen from some tourists. The estimated value of the ring is about twelve thousand dollars, one hundred forty-four thousand pesos."

Luis visibly started. His mouth was dry. "Why, that's a fortune!"

The inspector nodded. "A lot of money. We have reason to believe one of the Indians from that village took it." He watched Luis steadily. "There is a reward, offered by the insurance company, half the price of the ring."

Luis sensed a trap. For the barest fraction of a second he considered telling the inspector about the jewel and collecting the reward. But everyone knew that only police collect rewards, and anyone who protested was beaten, charged with a crime and thrown in jail. The instant passed and Luis said nothing.

The inspector continued. "The tourists were killed at the bend just below the village."

Luis shrugged. "They drive too fast, all of them."

The inspector lowered his voice confidentially. "It is not generally known, and you will understand how bad it would be for the tourist business, but the travelers were not killed accidentally, they were shot." The pause that followed was a dramatic one. "The ring is our only clue to the identity of the murderer."

Now Luis saw the jaws of the trap. His nebulous fear of the police became concrete. He thought of how close he had come to telling the inspector about the jewel. If he had been that foolish, he would not only have been cheated out of the reward, but connected in some way with the murder. The police had brutal ways of solving a case. Perhaps they planned to hold him, to torture him. No matter what happened he could no longer afford to tell them about the stone.

Inspector Menendes sighed. "Well, we're sorry we bothered you. We can't overlook any possibilities. You will find that we also took the liberty of searching your room. Desperate cases, desperate measures. I'm sure you understand." The inspector stood up. "Sergeant Roberto will show you out. If you think of anything, anything at all that might have a bearing, come to see us."

"I can find my own way, thank you," Luis said as the sergeant opened the door. As he walked down the corridor quickly, eager to be away, he felt as if the mind of the inspector were still following him—a strange Indian with eyes that seemed to probe his inner thoughts and an educated voice that contrasted eerily with his ungainly appearance.

Safely outside in the street, the inspector's aura evaporated and Luis' confidence returned. Surely if the police suspected him, they would not have let him go. He thought of the jewel, the immense fortune it represented. He weighed the risks and wondered whether he could recover it.

The desire for the emerald would not leave him. As he

53

sat in his favorite restaurant eating chicken and rice, it grew stronger than ever. To think that a little stone like that, scarcely bigger than a postage stamp, could be worth so much money. The warm food in his stomach and a glass of strong wine restored his confidence completely. In the face of the emerald's great worth, any risks involved in its recovery were minimized.

"It is only a matter of getting into the Villa," Luis decided. "And I can always go to see Carmelita." But simultaneously he recalled her searing flash of anger, his own resolution to break with her completely. "What if she has talked of our quarrel? What if I can't get through the gate?"

He finished his meal quickly, wondering what he should do. It had grown dark outside and the restaurant, now brightly lighted, had filled with diners. A tall, slender woman sat down at the table in front of him. In her thick, dark hair she was wearing an attractive comb, and the sparkling ornament suggested a solution to Luis' uncertainties. He would buy a comb for Carmelita and take it to the Villa Serena. Even though he had not visited her for several days, even if she had mentioned their quarrel to the gatekeeper, the gift would make him welcome. Once he was on the grounds, he would find a way to recover the stone.

Fleetingly he thought of the awesome image of the inspector, then scornfully dismissed it. The man was, after all, just an Indian and could see only what lay on the surface. He could not know, as Luis did, that the jewel was in the possession of a tourist staying at the villa or that Luis was going after it.

eight

FOLLOWING the guide's directions, Jessie easily found the Villa. The Villa Serena was built on the site of an old monastery. Over a century before, the building had been destroyed by fire, but the wall which enclosed the sloping grounds still stood, its rough stone covered with a mealy, yellow plaster, its top encrusted by jagged pieces of colored glass. A heavy, wooden gate had once helped to protect the beautiful gardens, but in the thirties when the land was auctioned by the state, the gate was no longer in existence and the grounds were no longer beautiful.

The wealthy merchant who bought the property was determined to have the most magnificent villa in the area. He started by restoring the gardens. Only the large, rare trees were left. The rank growth was stripped away and underneath, treasures of landscaping were found: stone walks that wandered down the slope, small fishponds, a miniature waterfall. Virile new plants were brought in to replace the old. Great masses of wild orchids were shipped in from the jungles to the south; rare bulbs were ordered from Europe; the walks and fishponds were repaired; a massive oak-slab gate with antique fittings was designed for the wall.

At the bottom of the slope, on the site of the old monastery, the merchant built his villa. Before it was finished, however, the work stopped abruptly. Through an error of judgment he was persuaded to back an ambitious general who promised, in return, leases to the rich, nationalized oil lands. Had the coup succeeded the merchant would have indeed been very, very rich, but the incipient revolution was aborted, and facing both ruin and disgrace, he hanged himself from one of the ancient rosewood trees.

His sinful body was not placed in consecrated ground but buried alone at the corner of the estate under an inconspicuous marker. His heirs could neither afford to finish the villa nor find a buyer for it because of its malodorous reputation. The estate was said to be haunted and on starless nights, the story went, the body of the merchant could be seen swinging from the branches of the fatal tree.

It was a half decade before a lonely Michigan widow, attracted by its reasonable price, decided to convert the villa into a hotel. Two rambling wings were attached to the main building, a parking area was built outside the main wall, and an excellent chef was found.

When the villa was finally ready to operate, it could accommodate only twenty-eight guests. But in spite of its limited capacity and the difficulties of operating a hotel in a foreign country, Ruth Alexander was moderately successful. She overcame the difficulty of finding servants by importing help from the northern border who did not know the local superstitions. She trained them to cater to a North American clientele, paid them well, and they remained with her. Even after fifteen years in Mexico, she retained her identity, speaking flawless Spanish with a flat, Midwestern accent.

Like the other tourists who came to the Villa, Jessie felt immediately at home with Mrs. Alexander. The tall, angular woman who greeted her was someone from her own familiar world. She realized suddenly that throughout her long flight from Dan she had been not only dislocated but frightened by the foreign surroundings.

Everything about the Villa Serena reassured her. Mrs. Alexander's brisk, friendly efficiency, the magnificent expanse of gardens, the immaculate room with tile fireplace and bath, the unobtrusive porter who carried in her bag and refused a tip.

"If you like the service, at the end of your stay you'll find a tip box in the lounge," Mrs. Alexander explained. "We find it more equitable to divide the money evenly. Cocktails are at seven, we eat at seven-thirty. Just follow the walk to the main building. I hope you'll be comfortable."

"I'm sure I will be. It's so beautiful here, I feel that I could stay forever."

Ruth Alexander turned back from the door with a smile. "I know. I did!"

Perhaps it was really the enchantment of the place, perhaps it was only that she was emotionally too tired to worry her problem any longer, but Jessie did feel that here was the peace she needed so desperately to find.

She sat by the window, seeing at first only the brilliance of the more flamboyant flowers and shrubs; then she noticed the creeping clusters of delicately pale wildflowers that climbed the gray, gnarled trunks of the trees, the pool covered with lily pads, the small birds that swooped, twittering, down to the birdbath.

Automatically she thought, "Dan would have liked all this." But she pushed the vagrant image of him into the recesses of her mind and locked her consciousness against it.

Now rays from the setting sun crept past the trees to tint the walks, the shrubs, the wall, all with the same golden hue. Then the brilliant light faded, and, as if that were a cue, the sleepy drone of insects began. A bullfrog jumped with a noisy splash into the pool. The first star

57

twinkled timidly overhead. Someone was lighting lanterns along the slope. A cool breeze sprang up, bringing with it the peppery scent of eucalyptus and the faint, distant sounds of activity in the main lounge.

And once again, Dan, like an unruly jack-in-the-box, popped up to remind her how difficult it was to enter a room of strangers alone. She pictured a formal dining room, another solitary meal like the ones that had preceded it along her route, and dreaded the approaching ordeal. "You must face things squarely," Jessie told herself severely. "Dan doesn't want you. You will have to do things in the future without him. And there's no time like the present to start."

To give herself courage she put on her new blue linen dress. It had been an extravagance, expensive and well cut with a soft color that brought out the cameo whiteness of her skin. It was, she decided, very becoming, and the handknit stole that matched it was not only attractive but warm.

Outside the lounge she could hear the buzz of voices, the clink of glasses, and was momentarily overcome by stage fright. Then, much as a swimmer plunges into icy water, she walked briskly into the room full of strangers.

It was not as she had pictured it, with intimate groups clustered together, but more like a suburban house party, where the guests, knowing only the host and hostess, make an effort to be congenial. There was a blazing fire in the stone fireplace. People were everywhere and all seemed to be talking at once. Discreet white-coated boys were filling and refilling glasses.

Ruth Alexander, in flowing brown chiffon, met Jessie at the door. Part of her success stemmed from a gift for knowing which people would get along well together. That afternoon she had observed Jessie's shyness, her quiet air of hurt withdrawal, and now she introduced her to the noisiest group in the room.

A tall, rangy man with graying hair and a lean, tanned face offered Jessie his seat by the fire.

"Mrs. Prewitt, this is Mr. Burton, an engineer," Mrs. Alexander said, "and our school teachers, Rose Fanning and Emily Allen. They've been vacationing in Mexico City."

"Not exactly vacationing—we spent the summer at the University." It was Emily, the smaller of the teachers, round, pale with alert, intelligent eyes like those of an inquisitive squirrel. "Rose wanted to perfect her Spanish, and I'm just curious."

There were other introductions, to an archaeologist, tall, handsome and completely bald, to a tweedy woman who was apparently his assistant, to a family with teenage youngsters who were planning to leave for Acapulco in the morning. Later Jessie could remember only their faces, not their names.

The archaeologist was talking about early Mayan development of hieroglyphics and the use of paper. The engineer mentioned a strange mask that had been found on his reclamation project, and the two men became involved in a comparison of the divergences and similarities of Indian cultures.

Someone asked Jessie which way she was headed, and because she really didn't know, she said vaguely, "South, eventually I'm going south." She was holding a cocktail glass by now, a refreshing, chilled mixture of pineapple and rum, and sipping it gave her the beginning of confidence.

"Oh, you just came in?" It was the other schoolteacher, a large woman with tightly curled reddish hair and a wide, friendly mouth.

"Yesterday, through Laredo. I took the new road from Monterrey. They tell me it's much shorter."

"Then you must have seen the wreck."

"What wreck?"

"Two Americans were killed, murdered, between here and Monterrey. I heard it on the radio."

"Not murdered, Rose," her friend corrected quietly. "Just killed."

Rose's face flushed with indignation. "It said the police suspected foul play. What more do you want?"

"Just the facts, Rose," Emily replied. Her dry, emotionless voice cut across a sudden lull in the conversation.

For some reason the engineer found her comment very funny and both teachers glared at him as he sputtered with suppressed laughter. "I'm sorry, ladies," he said apologetically. "Something in my throat."

It wasn't until she shared a table with them at dinner that Jessie realized that the teachers and Ralph Burton were old friends. By the time coffee was served Jessie felt that she had always known these delightful people, and they, in turn, casually extended their circle to include her, companionably calling her "Jessie" and inviting her to join them for an evening of bridge.

nine

FROM his post at the gate, Uncle Pedro watched the Villa. He could see someone moving in the lounge. That would be Juan, setting up the card tables and adding a log to the fire. Soon dinner would be over. After a while the *turistas* would go to bed and then Uncle Pedro could close the gate and lock it with the massive, old-fashioned bolts.

Although he was old, Uncle Pedro was very strong; besides, he kept a large club leaning against the gatepost where it would be handy. He had never used the club, but sometimes he would pick it up and swing its reassuring weight. Once there had been trouble when he failed to recognize a late-returning guest, but that was long ago when he was still new at the Villa. Nowadays he knew the room and face of every guest. He took his duties very seriously and prided himself that, while he was there, no stranger would pass. Luis Pérez, however, was no stranger. Often the guide came to take *turistas* to the cathedral or into the hills to the villages. He brought guests for rooms, too, and that was very kind of him. Uncle Pedro knew that the Señora Alexander paid money for bringing the *turistas*, but wasn't that as it should be? Luis was not a rich man, and surely a man must be paid for his labor. Besides, Luis was courting his niece Carmelita, and in these days it took much money to marry.

Luis would make a fine husband. Not everyone could

read and write or have a white card from the Department of Tourism. Carmelita was young and headstrong. Often she and Luis quarreled, but she seemed not to care. She would only shrug her narrow shoulders and purse her saucy lips as if to say, "There are many, many fish in the ocean." Too sure of herself, that one, too sure. And maybe she was right. Always Luis came back.

As if thought alone had materialized him, Luis came walking across the parking lot to the gate. Just as Uncle Pedro imagined him, he was wearing, even on this warm night, his belted camel's-hair coat.

"It's been a long time, Luis," the old man said, drawing out his pipe and preparing for a visit.

"Only a few nights, Uncle, I've been busy—besides, your niece has the temper of a hellcat. It does her good to cool off now and then."

Uncle Pedro nodded sagely. "Just like her mother, God rest her soul."

Luis lighted a match for the old man's pipe.

"Don't throw it near the cars, it's dangerous."

"No, Uncle." Luis nodded toward the parking lot. "Did a woman come here today in a white car?"

"A small woman, North American? Not so young? With pale-brown hair?"

"That's the one."

"Yes, she's here. Not very rich—she had only one suitcase." He reconsidered. "But it was a big one."

"I sent her. I hope you gave her a good room."

"One of the best. Near the fishpond."

"Oh, number twenty-three? That's a nice room."

"Number twenty-three is for two people; we put her in number twenty-four."

"Are they finished with dinner down there?"

"Pretty soon now. Carmelita will have to clear the tables." He added tolerantly, "It's hard to wait when you are young."

"I haven't seen her for many days, and though she has a bad temper, she has the face of an angel."

"It is always so." The old man sighed.

"Well, I will go down to the kitchen door and wait for her." And following his usual custom, Luis walked directly into the garden and started down the slope toward the lounge. However, as soon as he was safely away from the lighted gate, he turned off onto the stone walk that led to the fishpond.

Here there was only the silver incandescence of the moonlight to guide him. The huge, dark bushes and the night itself cloaked him with invisibility. Sounds from the main building were muted by distance, as if they belonged in another world. Along the walkway that led to the lounge, lanterns glowed feebly, making the surroundings even darker, more protective.

Near the pond Luis hesitated. It was not too late to turn back, to go to the inspector and tell him about the jewel and the North American woman who had it. But could he trust the police to share the reward with him? Would they not beat him and throw him in jail and keep the money for themselves? In his mind's eye the emerald shone with a thousand lights, but more brilliant than the stone was the green of dollars which even an illegal sale would bring.

An image of himself as a rich man skimmed across his mind. He could see himself driving a long car, married, perhaps to a girl with a fine house in Mexico City or maybe even to one of the rich *turistas* with slim, exciting legs and hair like honey. He was glad, now, that he hadn't married Carmelita. Although she was light skinned and beautiful with full, ripe breasts, she was ignorant, born only to be a servant.

At the thought of Carmelita, he remembered that soon the maids would be coming to turn back the beds and light the fires. Without wasting another minute, he swiftly crossed the lighted walk and tried the door to number twenty-four.

It slid noiselessly open.

Inside, the room had a faint scent of violets and, when he used his pocket flash, it was as he had expected, extremely neat like the little woman herself. He examined the bathroom first: the medicine cabinet, a small carrying case of cosmetics. There was nothing there. Then he opened the closets and felt in the pockets of her coat. Nothing. He examined the suitcase. Nothing. Finally he tried the dresser, feeling in the corners, hurrying now because time was growing short, and in his haste he overturned a bottle of perfume and the spicy scent was unpleasantly sharp, almost overpowering.

He heard a door slam heavily and one of the maids in loose huaraches scuff along the walk. Moving with desperate haste, he looked under the pillows, the throw rugs, behind the mirror. Now the maid was in the next room singing softly to herself. In a few minutes she would be here. Frantically he reached up to feel along the moldings above the windows, above the door. The stone was not to be found.

At the last possible second he dashed out of the room and across the lighted strip to hide in the bushes near the pond. The maid came out of number twenty-three and stood silhouetted against the lighted room, her head cocked as if she were listening. She approached the perimeter of the little pool, peering into the darkness while he stood rigid, not daring to breathe. His heart sounded like a trip hammer in his ears. It was incredible that she couldn't hear it. But she turned back, snapped out the light in twenty-three and, singing once again, entered the room he had just left.

Only now that the danger had passed did he taste the full bitterness of failure. Not to find the jewel was bad enough, but to know where it was and not to be able to get his hands on it—that was worse. For if the emerald was not in the room, it could only be in the tobacco pouch with the other stones still lying unnoticed at the bottom of the woman's handbag.

He considered remaining in the bushes until she came to bed. Perhaps if he told her he had sold her the wrong bag of stones, she would return them. No, it would never happen that way. More likely she would scream for the police.

His hopes of being rich, of having a fine house in Mexico City flickered and faded. Without the jewel there could be no house, no wife with exciting legs and hair that shone like spun honey. There could only be endless days of catering to tourists—and someone like Carmelita.

Later, sitting on the moonlit slope with her dark head on his lap, though he stroked the cool smoothness of her skin and cupped his hands over the ripeness of her breast, Luis knew Carmelita would never be enough. Life offered better things to Luis Pérez. The stone and the riches it would bring were rightfully his. He had bought it from the Indian, he had paid one hundred pesos for it, and he was determined to have it.

Carmelita looked up at him, her large, doe eyes velvety black. "What are you thinking of, *querido?*" she asked.

"Only of you, my dove," he murmured and leaned down to kiss her warm, moist lips, his eyes staring past her to the bulk of the Villa, amorphous and indistinct in the darkness. There, behind the dimly lit ribbon of walkways, one by one the bedroom lights were snapped out leaving only the main building shining brightly into the night. There, through the large, square windows of the lounge he could clearly see the little señora seated at a card table and although he could not see the pocketbook, he was sure that it was beside her.

ten

THE YOUNG POLICEMAN on the night desk was bored with
his magazine. It was only seven o'clock and a long, empty
evening stretched ahead. For a while he continued to leaf
through the pages, but nothing captured his interest.
Twice he opened the desk drawer to look at the fat,
brown envelope Inspector Menendes had left for the
commandant of police. Finally he took it from the
drawer, studied the large red "Confidential" stamped
across the front, hesitated a moment, turned it over and
ran his finger across the sealed flap.

If Inspector Menendes had not stamped the envelope
"Confidential," it might have reached the commandant
intact, but the young policeman was not only bored, he
was also ambitious. Like everyone else at the station, he
knew that the inspector worked only on tourist matters,
and cases involving tourists that were important enough
to be stamped "Confidential" were very serious indeed.

After six months on the desk, it sometimes seemed to
him that he would be there forever, that he would never
save enough money to buy a motorcycle or a place on
the Traffic Squad. His salary was small with rarely a
chance to augment it. The few extra pesos he earned each
evening by allowing the local reporter to examine the
police blotter added up to a very small *mordida*.

Very, very carefully he worked the flap loose, took the

papers out and read the duplicate file on the Randall murder. This was more interesting than he had expected, a valuable news item that the local reporter could easily sell to the wire services. Estimating its worth, the young policeman decided that seventy pesos would be a fair figure.

Still, as he slipped the papers back into the envelope, he wondered whether it was safe to sell the information. He thought uneasily of Inspector Menendes, the dark, flat features that seemed, like the powerful body, to be carved of rock. He pictured the inspector's eyes venomous with anger, and he decided to compromise, to sell only that part of the information that could not be traced directly to him.

Not far from the police station Inspector Menendes and Sergeant Roberto were drinking *cerveza* and eating hard, spicy sausages in a cramped, dark *cantina*. For the inspector it was a relaxing interlude. The scene that he had avoided with Theresa in the morning would be waiting for him tonight intensified by the delay, and he dreaded going home.

It was quiet in the *cantina*. Undecorated except for a single, neglected rubber plant and a colorful poster of a famous matador, it attracted few customers. Those who came stayed only briefly. The two men were able to sit undisturbed at one of the small marble-topped tables in the rear.

At eight o'clock the bartender obligingly turned up the radio so that they could hear the news and when it was over the inspector optimistically decided that he had at least one more day before word of the Randall murder would break.

"It's like getting a reprieve," he said expansively. "These tourist matters are explosive. You hope you can clear them up before the fireworks start."

Although they hadn't planned to stay, he ordered an-

67

other beer. He was tired. It was pleasant to drink the cold, bitter liquid and talk shop. "I went through it once before when that elderly widow disappeared at Lake Pazcuaro."

"I think I read about that," the sergeant said. "An Indian boy came for her in the evening and she went off with him somewhere."

The bartender brought them two more frosty bottles of beer and a small dish of peanuts. The inspector waited until he left, and then continued. "He wasn't exactly a boy. The maid who opened the door said he was a young man. It was dark. She didn't see his face clearly and she didn't recognize him. He said the señora expected him. And, sure enough, almost at once, she came down, left with the man and disappeared. Phttt." The inspector flicked his fingers as if, like a magician, he himself had made the woman vanish.

"They never found her at all?"

"Just her hat, floating on the lake near the island. But the fishermen claim that none of the boats were out. It was a bright summer night and they insisted they would have known. She was staying at the hotel with her niece, but the niece knew nothing—just that her aunt had been acting peculiar, secretive, for several days, that as soon as the gate bell rang, she ran down the stairs without saying a word."

"And what about the man?"

"The niece didn't know who he could be. They both spoke Spanish and often visited with strangers, people who worked in the shops or the fishermen, she said. They didn't always go out together; as a matter of fact they hadn't seen each other that day until dinner."

"You retraced her steps, of course."

"Yes, but it came to nothing. We couldn't find her or the man, whoever he was."

The sergeant shook his head in bewilderment. "It sounds like a corker."

"It was," the inspector agreed. "Of course, we had our theories, but we couldn't prove them. We thought perhaps she was murdered somewhere along the lake. She wore a lot of inexpensive jewelry that might have seemed valuable to someone who didn't know. We dragged the lake, found nothing. Her body could have caught in the weeds somewhere. . . . But without a body, do you have a murder? The niece stayed at Pazcuaro for several weeks. . . . Then she left for the States. For a while there was a lot of excitement about it and finally it died down." He shrugged and added, "It was an interesting puzzle. . . . It still is. . . ."

The sergeant waited, as if he had expected something more.

The inspector laughed. "We can't solve them all," he said. "Let's have another *cerveza*. This time I'll let you buy."

While they were talking a tourist in a wrinkled, gray suit wandered in from the street. Somewhere along the line he had picked up a woman. She looked like a gypsy with long, dark hair that fell down her back, a gaudy hand-painted skirt, gold earrings and a skin that was deep olive. The woman kept twining herself around the tourist and he was smiling a drunken, varnished smile and balancing himself on the balls of his feet to keep from tottering. The woman ordered a bottle of rum, took the man's wallet to pay for it, put the wallet back in his pocket and led the drunken man out into the street.

The inspector nodded toward the retreating back. "There's a guy who really needs help. We do what we can to protect the tourists, but just what can we do? They're too rich, too careless. When they get into trouble they scream to the authorities."

The sergeant agreed indifferently. "He's asking for it. If that woman robs him he has no right to complain."

"But he will, that's the point. Mexico needs the tourists. It's a serious matter. We can't afford to have them robbed or cheated. Yet too many Mexicans, especially those who live by the tourist trade, regard the North Americans as natural prey. Like that guide and his worthless stones."

The sergeant, unconsciously impressed by Luis' rich coat and gold watch, found himself defending him. "The guide's all right. He does a job like any other job. So he sells some junk to the tourists. They'll buy it somewhere else. A man must live."

The inspector sipped his beer, then shook his head. "A guide? Who needs a guide here? In the capital, yes. San Luis, no!"

Still the sergeant disagreed. "Maybe there's not much to see. But the tourists come. They can't speak the language. They're happy to have someone help them. I saw it myself this afternoon. A *turista* gave that guide fifty pesos, imagine that, fifty pesos just for telling her where to stay."

"Fantastic! And he'll collect another ten pesos from the hotelkeeper for sending her there. I could be wrong. I didn't like him or anything about him. You saw his eyes when I mentioned the value of the ring? If he'd bought it from one of the Indians do you think he'd turn it over to the police, even to preserve his own job? And believe me, Sergeant, if we don't arrest that murderer, it will affect his job. Do you think tourists will drive down from Monterrey if they think it's open season on them?"

The two men drank in silence for a while. The bartender stopped polishing glasses and turned on the hourly news. First there was a long, dramatic commercial, then the newscaster's voice, detached and factual. . . . A disastrous earthquake had occurred in Morocco. . . . A plane was missing over Uruguay, thirty-seven persons were aboard. . . . The Chinese on the mainland were shelling the Chinese on the island. . . . And then, "Two United States citizens were killed yesterday afternoon on the new Mexico City highway. The tourists, Mr. and Mrs. Randall, were shot as they drove toward San Luis."

When the broadcast was finished, the pleasure had gone out of their evening. The inspector was deflated.

"Well, that's it," he said gloomily. "We couldn't have kept it quiet much longer anyway. All hell will break loose tomorrow."

"Can anything be done?"

The inspector looked tired suddenly. "Nothing, just take it as it comes. We might requisition another man to take care of complaints and reports. We can expect some newsmen from the States. Before we're through we'll be accused of everything in the book, from shielding the criminals to robbing the dead." He stood up slowly as if his big body had become too heavy for him to manage. "Come on, Sebastián, let's go home."

It was the first time the inspector had ever used his given name and Sergeant Roberto was inordinately pleased.

He was no longer working *for* the inspector but *with* him. The inspector's problems became his. He was, all at once, personally aware of the pressures that would result from the news break.

Unexpected compensations came with the evil wind of mischance. The premature announcement of the Randall murder that would complicate the inspector's job subtly worked to make his personal relationships easier. It formed a bridge between him and the sergeant and it affected Theresa, too.

She heard the news in her bedroom where she was brooding over her husband's strange "Indian behavior." His sullen silence at the party had been inexcusable. He

71

had insulted all of their friends and neighbors and even the priest. Then, without any explanation or apology to their guests, he had left with that sergeant. As if that wasn't bad enough, when he did come home he slept on the couch. He hadn't said "Goodbye" to her in the morning. All day she had waited, but he hadn't telephoned. Now he was late again.

The more Theresa nourished his offenses against her, the more hostile she became.

Her mother had warned her against marrying an Indian. "He may be educated," her mother had said, "but he was brought up among savages who don't treat their wives as civilized men do."

How right her mother was. Her husband was not like the other men she knew. He had no concern for the social niceties. He was embarrassingly outspoken against the church. Because of his work the neighbors were all a little afraid of him. Everything he did isolated her from the world around her and now, on top of that, he had proved himself to be callous and indifferent, leaving her purposely alone.

Instead of keeping some warm food for him as she usually did when he was delayed, immediately after María was in bed she washed the dishes, prepared a sandwich, left it on the kitchen table and retreated again to her bedroom.

There she lay listening to the radio. The wistful Spanish songs of unrequited love increased her melancholy. She felt rejected, unwanted, and the tears fell down her plump cheeks and soaked into the pillow. "I won't even speak to him," she decided vindictively. "Let him sleep on the couch if he likes it so well out there."

She was so absorbed in her grievances that she almost missed the news. It was the word "tourists" that attracted her attention. "Mr. and Mrs. Randall were shot as they drove to San Luis," the announcer said. "It is believed that they were murdered, then robbed of a valuable ring and a large sum of money. Inspector Menendes of the Tourist Investigative Office expects to make an arrest shortly."

Theresa was shocked out of her self-absorption. She couldn't remember when she had been so excited. Imagine hearing her husband's name on the radio! For a few seconds she tried to recapture the attitude of hurt withdrawal, but pride and curiosity interfered. She could picture the women in the courtyard clustering around her for details and the condescension with which she would supply them. She saw herself in her best black dress carrying herself with aloof dignity as the wife of an inspector should. This case would show them all that even if he had behaved badly at the party, her husband was a man of importance.

Quickly Theresa washed her tear-stained face, powdered her nose, put on her best flowered robe and returned to the kitchen. There she economically wrapped the sandwich and put it away for lunch.

By the time the inspector arrived at the apartment she had a pot of beans and meat heating on the stove, the table was set and she stopped patting *tortillas* long enough to give him a welcoming smile.

eleven

Luis didn't hear the news broadcast until the next morning. All evening he was with Carmelita in the gardens of the Villa Serena, listening to her chatter, stroking her thick cloud of hair and wondering how to recover the jewel. She told him a long, involved story of a quarrel with one of the other maids, and her voice, which once he had found so soothing, now interfered noisily with his concentration. Still, since she was his entry to the Villa, he dared not offend her and he automatically answered with endearments that seemed to satisfy her.

He continued to hope that somehow luck would be with him and that the jewel would fall into his hands. He was convinced by now that the fortune it represented was rightfully his and that it would be restored to him. He kept his eyes on the entrance to the lounge waiting for the little woman to return to her room, but the hours passed. Other lights all over the Villa had winked out. The crickets had fallen silent. Only a few night birds still bravely called to one another from the trees. It grew colder. Carmelita was murmuring uncomfortably. He covered her with his warm, tan coat and she snuggled back with her head in his lap and at last fell asleep. The lounge remained lighted; the *turista* did not come out.

Luis toyed with the idea of speaking to her, of offering his services as a guide, but it would be difficult to explain his presence on the grounds so late at night. He considered again simply asking for the return of the stones. He could explain that he had made a mistake, that they were already promised to someone else. Luis' devious mind rejected this scheme as utterly impractical. Judging by his own reactions he knew that she would never return them. She would immediately be certain that she had made a rare bargain and she would most carefully examine her purchase. Above all he didn't want the woman to examine the contents of the tobacco pouch. As long as she was unaware that she had the emerald, he had a good chance of getting it.

Finally the door of the lounge opened. He could see the woman clearly silhouetted against the light. But he was still without a plan, and he sat on the slope miserably watching as she and the tall man with her walked along the wing to her door. In the silence he could hear their footsteps clearly on the stone walk and the man's voice as he said, "Don't forget, Jess, the Plaza, at noon." He heard her door close, the click of the man's lighter as he stopped to light a cigarette, and then his footsteps as he moved on further down the wing.

The little señora's shadow flickered just once across the luminated patch of her window while Luis watched and waited, still hoping to think of a way to reach her.

Inside the cheerful room Jessie was completely unaware that anyone was watching her. She was filled with the pleasant aftertaste of the evening and anticipation of her lunch with Ralph Burton the next day. Everything at the Villa was wonderful; the room itself, warmed by the embers of a fire built in her absence, seemed to welcome her. Momentarily the heavy scent of her perfume disturbed her and drew her to the empty bottle, but annoyance could not penetrate her mood of enchanted contentment. She dismissed the spilled perfume as a maid's careless accident . . . remote . . . and like the rest of her problems, unimportant. Quickly, sleepily, she undressed, turned out the light and went to bed.

And now the entire Villa lay in darkness. It would be easy, Luis thought, to wait another hour, until the señora fell asleep, then crawl through her windows and steal the gem. But what would he do about Carmelita?

As if his thinking about her had awakened her, she opened her large, liquid eyes and murmured sleepily, "You'll have to go, Luis, Uncle Pedro will want to lock the gate."

The gate was already locked. Uncle Pedro was not to be found and Luis, who had never before stayed so late at the Villa, wondered uncomfortably how he would leave. But Carmelita, without difficulty, slid back the heavy bolts and the slab-oak gate swung noiselessly open on its oiled hinges. For a brief moment Carmelita pressed her firm body against his and kissed him passionately; then he was outside and he could hear her sliding the bolts back into place.

He thought of the simple lock mechanism. It was easier to leave the Villa, he decided, than to enter it.

It wasn't until Luis was walking through the deserted streets toward his room that it occurred to him that, maybe, after all, he would not get the jewel. He felt cheated, as if someone had stolen something from him.

It was a sensation that he'd often had as a child when he went shopping with his father, to the large grocery store that lay at the edge of the California town. For a small boy even the walk there was a long one. He could still see that store, the long shelves lined with food, the boxes of candy, the heavily iced cakes and cookies, and most enticing of all, the rack of toys: brightly painted airplanes and cars, puzzles, rubber balls, soldiers, all mysteriously packaged in cellophane and hanging from metal hooks. Every week Luis would look through all the bags, finally

76

select one, take it down and put it in his father's shopping basket.

On the way home carrying one of the heavy packages, he would dream of playing with the toy, but when the groceries were unpacked, it was never there. He was always disappointed, like someone who is the victim of a conjuring trick, certain that the toy was there, hurt and mystified at its disappearance.

In some ways his present frustration was the same. He had been so certain when he went to the Villa that he would return with the jewel that he couldn't resign himself to failure. He reached home discouraged and depressed, yet unable to abandon his dreams of wealth.

Because he was no longer a child, Luis forced himself dispassionately to review the situation. He had failed to recover the stone because he had assumed that it would be in the señora's room, and instead it was in the handbag that was always with her. Somehow he must find a way to take it from her. Perhaps violence would be required, but Luis was not a violent man and the thought frightened him. He preferred to rely on the shrewdness and luck that had always, in the past, worked to his advantage. In this situation luck seemed to be running against him, but the current would change. He would stay close to the señora, close to the jewel, and an opportunity would present itself.

During the night he slept poorly, tormented by dreams in which he, the inspector and the little señora were endlessly chasing each other. Shortly after dawn he awakened with his brain pulsing excitedly. In his dreams, during the endless chase, he had recovered the jewel. He lay for a few minutes, his eyes blinking against the soft morning light, not realizing at first that his dream had no reality. In his dream it had all seemed so easy that he tried to recapture the sequence of events and, little by little, they returned to him. All at once he was very excited. Divorced from the exaggerated, surrealistic surroundings of the dream a very simple way of recovering his treasure presented itself.

Since Luis knew nothing of the subterranean workings of his own mind, he believed that the solution had come to him by magic. It was therefore flawless, foolproof. It couldn't possibly fail. Within a few hours the emerald would be his. Suddenly he connected the jewel with the wealth the fortuneteller had prophesied for him. The idea came as a surprise, but it served to reinforce his faith in the dream. Hurriedly he climbed out of bed to check his horoscope, found the single word "Caution" and nodded in silent agreement. The plan, perfect as it was, would require caution.

Since it was still early he turned on the radio while he heated some strong, black coffee. There were a few bursts of martial music, two rapid commercials, then a digest of last night's news. At the mention of the ring and the announcement that the inspector intended, shortly, to make an arrest, he realized it could not be true. If the inspector were looking for a ring, he would search forever, for there was no longer a ring to find.

While he dressed, Luis hummed cheerfully. He drank several cups of the bitter coffee and smoked an equal number of cigarettes before he was ready to leave for the Plaza. Although it was still cool outside he decided not to wear his tan coat. Without it, in only dark slacks and a white sport shirt, he appeared slimmer, taller, different, as though he had discarded a uniform and were clad in civilian anonymity.

On the way to the plaza he stopped to buy a newspaper and a large bag of garishly colored gumdrops. The streets were crowded with early shoppers, but the square was still almost empty.

A few elderly people were warming themselves in the sun. Some very small children were racing around the

78

fountain while their mothers sat gossiping nearby. A policeman flirting with a pretty girl in a bright yellow dress was blocking the walk. A group of ragged, dirty boys were sprawled out on the grass talking together in high, cracked voices. Luis found an empty bench near them, sat down, opened his bag of candy and slowly ate a sticky, orange sweet. Then, as if he didn't notice the boys eyeing him greedily, he unfolded his newspaper and started to read.

twelve

THE DINING ROOM at the Villa was inviting in the morning light. The tables were set with the colorfully decorated pottery that had been used at dinner the night before, the linen was spotless, the flowers appeared to have just been picked. And the room was filled with the tantalizing aroma of freshly ground coffee and home-baked breads.

Jessie was the last one in for breakfast. She had slept late. At the instant of awakening she had been frightened, disoriented, but almost immediately her pleasant surroundings reassured her. She was cheerful, rested, and now, she realized, also ravenously hungry.

The room was almost empty, but from a table near the windows, the teachers called to her. Emily had been writing postcards and was wearing a pair of horn-rimmed glasses that seemed disproportionately large for her nose. She looked over the top of them at Jessie and smiled her approval.

"You look very nice this morning, Jess. We're almost finished, but you're welcome to join us."

"Thank you. The coffee smells wonderful."

Rose was already pouring her a cup. "It is. I think I'll have another cup, too."

Emily continued her writing. "If you will excuse me, I'll just finish these."

Rose was bubbling over with information. "The archaeologist left this morning. You should have seen him. Full tropical gear, kepi and all. Emily calls him the 'Yul Brynner of the Yucatán.'" Her friend glanced at her disapprovingly and Rose hurried on. "In private, of course. Emily never says anything unpleasant in public."

Jessie laughed with her and asked, "Have you heard any news? I've only been away from home two days, yet I seem to have lost touch with everything."

"Nothing exciting. The President made a speech last night, and, oh yes, those Americans that were killed just north of here were actually murdered. Shot, it said on the radio. What was their name, Emily?"

Emily screwed the top on her pen and gave Rose a withering look. "Randall—but that's hardly breakfast conversation. Look at Jessie, she's as pale as a ghost."

"Nonsense. It's exciting, don't you think so?" Then noticing Jessie's shocked expression, she said contritely, "You didn't know them did you, Jess?"

Jessie shook her head. Perhaps it was only because the death of an American in a foreign country becomes personal to all other Americans; but for a moment, she felt as if she had known them, as if, in some odd way, their lives were entwined with hers.

"I'm sorry if I upset you, Jessie," Rose said humbly, pouring more coffee.

Jessie smiled. Her momentary identification with the Randalls had already passed. "It's nothing. I heard about the accident in Monterrey. They were talking about it at the hotel and it almost seemed to me as if I did know them. Well, what's good for breakfast?"

"The fresh pineapple is wonderful," Emily suggested, as she gathered up the postcards that were spread across the table. "We're going to a leather factory if you'd like to come. Otherwise, if you don't mind, we'd better get started."

"No, thank you," Jessie said. "I've some shopping to do and I'm meeting Ralph Burton for lunch."

Rose obviously wanted to make some comment on that, but with an effort said nothing. Docilely, as Emily rose, she did too and equally docilely followed her from the dining room.

After they had gone Jessie thought about the Randalls again, but without a recurrence of the sad sense of identification. It was too beautiful a day to be sad about anything. As if she had been let out of a box, she was acutely aware of the beauties of nature. Outside the vast windows the dew still lingered on the garden. In the shade it glistened so heavily on the grass that each blade might have been freshly painted a rich, dark green. In contrast with the grass, only the cannas shone brilliantly white, while the vivid colors of the other flowers appeared dimmed, delicately pastel. It was so unlike the view of the purple hills from her dining-room window at home that an inadvertent image of Dan crossed her mind.

"I should send him a telegram," she decided. "Tell him where I am, at least."

But like the death of the Randalls, thoughts of Dan were unpleasant and she brushed them aside. Instead she concentrated on a tiny hummingbird with an iridescent ruby throat who hovered near the cannas. And pleasantly insulated against both the future and the past, she leisurely finished her breakfast.

"Later," she decided. "I'll think of Dan later."

On her way through the lounge she stopped to chat with Mrs. Alexander, who was packing pottery into a huge carton. "You look as though you were moving," she said.

"No. My friend Ramón Morales is celebrating his birthday again," Ruth explained. "He chooses a date at random, borrows half of my servants and most of my dishes." Her smile softened the peevish words. "But it's always a nice party. I'm free to bring a few guests of my own. Why don't you come along, Jessie?"

"I'd like to go, if you're sure it's all right."

"Perfectly. Several of the others will be going. We'll leave right after cocktails. Ramón's house is well worth seeing. You might have noticed it on the main avenue coming out. A great, pink monstrosity set back from the road."

On the way to town Jessie looked for the Hacienda Morales, but she must have taken the wrong turn, for she ended up on one of the narrow, cobblestoned streets that the day before she had found so depressing. Now she discovered that they were quaint and interesting. There were little open shops, restaurants no larger than cubbyholes, doors through which she could catch a glimpse of the fascinating courtyards filled with exotic flowers. She passed an open market piled high with produce, great bunches of bananas and oranges that grew only a few miles south.

After the narrow arterial, her first sight of the huge expanse of the Plaza was breathtaking. The ancient gray stone cathedral that flanked one side of the square rose massive and ornate, dwarfing everything around it so that the Plaza itself seemed merely an appendage, a private park, and the people on the walks seemed to be going either to or from the church.

Because it was not yet time to meet Burt, Jessie parked the car and explored the tiny shops in the area adjoining the Hotel Plaza. She drifted from window to window examining exquisite jewelry, delicately etched leather work, butterfly trays, weird tin masks. Then she was in front of the telegraph office and, hesitantly, went in.

An attractive girl with broad, Oriental cheekbones nodded encouragement from behind the counter. "Permit I help you, Señora."

83

"Can I send a telegram? In English, I mean."

"Of course, Señora."

Quickly, before she could change her mind, Jessie sent Dan a wire saying nothing more than where she was staying. Almost immediately she regretted it, as if that simple act were forcing her to a decision she was not yet able to make.

It was shortly before noon when she started across to the Plaza. A policeman at the crosswalk, standing very straight and tall in his black uniform, motioned her to cross the street. At the corner the snow-cone vendor, who was doing a brisk business in purple, red and green cones, held one out to her. He was a small man, very dark, with a great, black, comical mustache, and when Jessie pleasantly shook her head, he returned her a delighted smile. The gay cart of the snow-cone vendor gave the Plaza a festive air. The benches that lined the walks leading to the fountain were crammed with people. Women in voluminous clothes were watching children who ran whooping and hollering around them. Here and there the brilliant floral skirts of the dark-skinned girls attracted attention. An old man on one of the benches was reading a newspaper with thick bifocals and the aid of a large magnifying glass. Jessie, looking around for Ralph Burton, saw him come toward her from the fountain, moving with that purposeful manner which, in her mind, distinguished him.

At just that minute two small dogs ran across the walk in front of her, yipping as though someone had kicked them. Immediately after them raced a group of ragged boys screaming in high-pitched voices.

One of the boys bumped into Jessie as he passed and, without pausing, snatched the handbag from her arm. The boy was several yards ahead of her before she realized what had happened. He was looking back at her, with black, almond-shaped eyes in his urchin face and he ran right into Ralph Burton. The boy, still holding onto the purse, started screaming and kicking, but Burt didn't let him go. He held the youngster at arm's length and shook him as effortlessly as if he were a kitten.

A crowd collected. Within seconds the benches were deserted, the Mexicans gathering in a silent circle to watch the two North Americans and the kicking boy.

The boy had dropped the pocketbook. He was screaming abusively and squirming to get away. Tears were rolling down his cheeks, leaving light streaks in the dirt. Ralph Burton continued to hold him and shake him until he was silent, then asked him something in Spanish. The boy answered in a pouring jumble of words.

"He says some man put him up to it," Burt translated.

Perversely, now that she had her pocketbook back, Jessie felt sorry for the boy. The child's obvious fright touched her. She had an image of a dank jail cell and the diminutive felon seated on a cot, staring into nothingness. When she saw a policeman coming across the square toward them she insisted frantically, "Let him go, Burt. Please let him go. It doesn't matter. I've lost nothing."

Burt loosened his grip; and dropping to his hands and knees, the boy pushed his way through the legs of the crowd. Once away from the ring of people he started to run, a terrified little figure, heading for the rabbit warren in which he lived.

The policeman elbowed his way forward, unhurried, dignified, his mustache waxed to the same leathery shine as his boots. Slowly he opened a pad and started asking questions. Burt answered in fluid Spanish. Jessie heard her name, the Villa Serena, then the policeman started questioning people in the crowd. They all looked at him with cold, hostile eyes and shook their heads. Jessie gathered that the policeman was trying to learn the culprit's name, but apparently everyone denied knowing him. At last, with disgust, the officer elaborately closed his notebook and barked a short command which must have been the equivalent of "Break it up" because the people started to disperse, returning to the benches that lined the walks.

"Come on, Jess," Burt said, taking her arm. "You look as if you could use a drink."

He took her to the hotel bar across from the square. After the hot brightness of the street the bar was dim and cool with soft upholstered chairs that smelled of wax polish and new leather. There were no other customers. A large ugly parrot chained to a perch in the corner scratched his feathers, then peered around the room, screeching in a raucous, masculine voice, *"Buenas noches, Señor, Señora!"* The bartender and waiter played a noisy dice game at the end of the bar while the radio, tuned to the local station, alternated long, dramatic statements with occasional bursts of music that sounded to Jessie always like "Guadalajara."

"You should have let me turn that boy over to the police, Jessie," Burt insisted when they had their drinks.

"I couldn't. He was so small and scared."

"Maybe, but sooner or later he'll be caught at it again. He was hired, you know, to snatch your purse."

"You mean sort of like Fagin and Oliver Twist?"

"Something like that," Burt said dryly.

"But of all the people in the park, why me?"

"Because you're an American—and all Americans are rich. Didn't you know?"

"Well, I'm not rich, but I'd have been considerably poorer if he got away. But let's not talk about it. There's no harm done and I wouldn't want it on my conscience that I sent the little monster to jail."

They finished their drinks and had another. The bar began to fill up with tourists staying at the hotel. Several of them had apparently been to the market that morning and were talking about how dirty it was. The couple at the next table was discussing the Randall murder, the

86

woman insisting stubbornly: "I won't go back that way. No matter what you say, George, we're not going back that way."

When they left for lunch the room was packed. The parrot on his perch was busily screaming, *"Buenas noches, Señor, Señora!"* and above the din the radio was still playing "Guadalajara."

thirteen

THE DAY began much as the inspector predicted it would. Even before he arrived two reporters from the States were waiting on the bench at the police station. They were both unshaven and had obviously slept in their clothes. A number of telephone calls, all marked "urgent" or "extremely urgent," had accumulated at the switchboard. The phones kept ringing. The commandant had conveniently taken the day off to attend a vaguely identified "civic conference." The lieutenant in charge didn't know what to do with the calls and kept referring them back to the switchboard. The atmosphere in the station was guarded.

Sergeant Roberto was extremely nervous. He was afraid that the reporters would corner him, and he didn't know what to say. Like the rest of the policemen on duty he studiedly ignored them. Perched on the edge of the police desk where he could see the door, he tried to appear unconcerned. Because the sergeant was there, the officer at the desk could not take his typewriter out, and he looked mildly annoyed although he said nothing.

At his usual hour, as if today were no different from any other day, the inspector came through the large, barnlike front door. He had dressed with extra care. His stiff, black hair was brushed and shining with oil, his brown suit carefully pressed, his shoes highly shined. He was wearing a starched, white shirt and above the stiff collar his face looked more forbidding than ever. Except for the efforts he had made with his appearance there was no indication that he was braced for a difficult day. He was, however, well prepared. In his pocket was a skillfully edited press release.

The idea for writing it had come to him the evening before as he sat at the kitchen table telling Theresa about the murder. She had greeted him warmly. The storm he had expected had apparently blown over and she was insatiable for details. After he had given her the barest outline he was hard pressed to avoid those questions which touched on the sensitive areas of his investigation. So he dwelt on the technical facts, the approximate speed at which the Randalls were traveling, the angle at which the car hit the rocks, the police routine that uncovered the missing ring, the detailed description that had been given to the pawnshops. He told her everything and nothing. He filled his story with so many irrelevant details that to Theresa it seemed complete, and it was from this story that he designed his misleading report.

On the surface it appeared to have been conscientiously compiled, but in reality most of the essentials were missing. It failed to pinpoint the exact location of the accident or the proximity of the Indian village. It omitted any mention of the recovered bullets. Instead it emphasized that pawnshops throughout Mexico had been alerted and implied that it was through one of these that the police shortly expected to make an arrest.

This expurgated version of the investigation the inspector intended to make public. It probably would not stand an informed scrutiny, but he hoped it would shield his real objectives.

With ponderous dignity he walked past the reporters to the police desk and handed the officer the handwritten report. "Have some copies made for the press." His manner was so authoritative, brusque, that the officer instinctively jumped to attention. He only nodded to Sergeant Roberto, who, not knowing what else to do, followed the inspector across the station toward the courtyard that led to the government offices.

"There's a call coming in for you, Inspector Menendes," the switchboard operator shouted after him. "It's from Mexico City."

But the inspector did not seem to hear him.

The reporters did, however. As soon as they were aware that this was the Inspector Menendes for whom they had been waiting, they ran after him. They overtook him in the heat of the courtyard, displaying their press cards as though they were badges of privilege that allowed them to probe the secret areas of his mind.

Without stopping, the inspector courteously acknowledged their presence.

It might have been rehearsed. . . . the deliberate tread . . . the concentrated manner in which he cocked his head as if he were either slightly deaf or had only limited command of the English language.

When the reporters raised their voices the sergeant was secretly amused. He glanced at the inspector, noticed his air of bland attention as if he were trying to understand what the shouting was about.

The barrage of questions followed a pattern which was to become a familiar one in the succeeding hours.

"Exactly where did the murder take place?" . . . "At what time?" . . . "Why did the police think it was an accident?" . . . "What sort of gun fired the shot?" . . . "Do the police have the ring?" . . . "What steps are being taken to find the murderer?"

The inspector answered only those questions he wished to hear; the others he glossed over evasively. He was, however, patently co-operative until one of the men asked, "What is the government doing to protect the tourists?"

It was then that the characteristic flash of anger, which had so frequently overawed the sergeant, revealed itself. The inspector stopped abruptly. He seemed suddenly remote, imposing.

"Our government is concerned with the safety of everyone within our borders." His cold voice, his stilted use of the English language made the words sound like an official pronouncement. "We deeply regret the unfortunate death of the Randalls, but it is, after all, an isolated instance of violence."

It was incongruous to listen to him and watch him. As if he had assumed an extra dimension the inspector seemed awesome and unapproachable, drawn on a scale different from that of the other men. Even the reporters who were accustomed to rebuffs were reduced to speechlessness. When he started walking again they still followed, but they had no further questions to ask him.

With silent admiration Sergeant Roberto watched the subtle way in which Inspector Menendes had gained control of the situation. He was seeing the inspector with new eyes, wondering how much of the scene had been planned, how much had happened naturally.

Outside the office door the inspector hesitated briefly. He gave the men one of his rare, charming smiles. "I'm sorry, Señores, I have told you all I can. You will find a detailed report at the police desk. . . . Now, if you will excuse me, my telephone is ringing."

He brushed past the newsmen into the office, and the sergeant, still not certain what was expected of him, went in after him.

The inspector's face was flushed as he picked up the receiver; that was the only indication of tension. His voice was calm, decisive. "Inspector Menendes speaking. . . .

Yes, sir, we have spread a net for the ring." There was a pause during which he settled himself more comfortably in his chair. "No, that is not propaganda, we do expect to make an arrest shortly. . . . I'm sorry, sir, you'll have to let me handle this my own way or put someone else in charge."

He put down the receiver, wiped his forehead with a very large, very white handkerchief and looked at the sergeant as if to say, "You see how it is." Aloud he said, "Did you put a man near the village?"

"Yes. If anyone leaves we'll know it."

"Good." The inspector lapsed again into absorbed silence. At last he said, "There's nothing we can do but wait." Then he added with a dry chuckle, "You might send a copy of that press release to the Department of Tourism in Mexico City. Put it in the form of an official report, address it to the Chief Inspector, Investigative Division, and I'll sign it."

The telephone rang again. The inspector motioned for the sergeant to wait and picked up the receiver. "Inspector Menendes here. . . . Yes, Charles, I can see you at noon. . . . Lunch at the Hotel Plaza? . . . Right, twelve sharp."

"The United States consul," he said. "Can you have the car here before noon?"

Sergeant Roberto saluted smartly. "I'll have it here by eleven forty-five."

Accustomed to seeing the inspector only in relation to the San Luis police department, the sergeant had never before fully realized his superior's importance in the world outside. He was impressed by the telephone calls, by the luncheon invitation from the consul, by the fact that in spite of the seriousness of the situation the Mexican government relied on the inspector to resolve it. But what had the most effect on the sergeant's imagination was the inspector's resourcefulness. He seemed to have anticipated all of the exigencies and allowed none of them to deflect him from his charted course. In the midst of the confusion he moved with assurance toward his own predetermined objectives.

The inspector, however, was not as self-confident as he appeared to be. Every once in a while he suffered a pang of doubt. He was waging a campaign of deception against his superiors in the capital. He was issuing misleading information to the press. He intended, deliberately, to deceive his friend, the United States consul, all because he was so certain that he was right. But what if he was wrong?

His theory that an Indian from the village was the murderer was the only one consistent with the facts. The ring would not turn up until the criminal felt free of suspicion, and therefore he must not, accidentally, be alerted. Yet, what if by one of those unpredictable freaks of chance there was an additional factor, unknown and unweighed? Someone like the guide who had been traced and dismissed as guiltless. Could anyone else have been involved? A passing motorist, perhaps, who robbed the bodies? It was one of the unmeasurable elements in a murder case. It seemed unlikely, yet it must be considered, and the knowledge that pawnshops throughout Mexico were watching for the ring was reassuring.

Still the inspector clung to his original theory. The ring must be hidden near the village, and no rumor of suspicion must alarm the Indians or it would remain hidden forever.

Shortly before noon the sergeant brought the car to the front of the building. There was an added respect in the way he opened the rear door and stood at rigid attention as the inspector climbed in, as if he understood the need for maintaining the inspector's impressive dignity.

. . . And the inspector, in the back seat, marveled at the sergeant's perception and congratulated himself on the choice of an assistant.

On the way to the hotel he again started shifting the pieces of the puzzle. He toyed with the idea of discussing the situation frankly with the consul. He imagined himself saying, "We know it's one of the Indians, but even in Mexico we can't arrest an entire village." But he knew he wouldn't say it. He would give the consul the same carefully contrived fiction he had sent to his own superior. The most discreet officials had been known to make ill-advised statements, and although Inspector Menendes would have liked to protect himself by sharing his theory, he wanted more to expose the murderer. To do that, he had to have time to find the ring.

They had emerged from the shady side streets into the glare of the open Plaza. The streets were almost deserted, but in the square itself a crowd had collected. The people were pushing each other, craning their necks to see over the shoulders in front of them. Even the familiar figure of the snow-cone vendor was circling the perimeter of the crowd looking for an opening, his stand untended and unpatronized. A policeman was approaching from the direction of the church.

"I wonder what's happening there," the inspector said.

"Shall I stop and find out?" Without waiting for an answer the sergeant started to pull the car over toward the curb.

"No, we can't stop. We're late now. Anyway the police are already there."

fourteen/

FROM HIS BENCH on the Plaza, Luis saw the police car pulling in to the curb with Sergeant Roberto at the wheel and the inspector perched, like a monstrous toad, on the back seat. He had a fleeting recurrence of the feeling that the inspector's mind was able to follow him and that his presence here was not accidental. It was a sensation based partly on Luis' knowledge of his own guilt and partly on conditioning that extended back into the mists of childhood.

In California the illegal immigrants who worked in the vineyards lived under an ever-present threat of deportation. Their presence was known and tolerated only so long as there was no open conflict with the law. Whatever the working conditions, whatever the injustices, the Mexican laborers dared not protest; and Luis' parents, like the others, lived in constant fear that they would be driven away from the place that had become their home.

When he grew older Luis rebelled against those fears and through his rebellion created the realization of them, but while he was still small the police were a faceless, all-powerful authority that controlled his parents' decisions. Once, during the harvest, they had taken Luis with them to the vineyards. He had helped pick the ripe red grapes, eating the prettiest ones, piling the rest into buckets. By evening his arms were lame from carrying the heavy buckets, his mouth sore from the acid sweetness of the fruit, yet to the child it had been a holiday. He had enjoyed the companionship of the adults, the crispness of the autumn air, the musty scent of the grapes, and best of all the pride of doing a man's work. He begged to be allowed to continue in the fields, and although his parents were willing enough, the overseer had refused.

"You must go to school, Luis," he had said. "Here everyone goes to school."

Luis' father protested. "What good is reading to a poor man? We are very poor."

The overseer shook his head. "No, he must go to school or there will be trouble with the police."

And so Luis had returned to school. Those were the words, he learned, that decided everything, "trouble with the police." When their neighbor Juan García beat his wife there was "trouble with the police." Men had come and taken Juan away and later his parents had talked in whispers about it. When Luis stole the car his mother beat him with a broom, crying over and over, "Now you've done it! Made trouble for us with the police!"

Her anguished, frightened voice returned to him as he sat in the Plaza wondering what had gone wrong, how he had been drawn into this dangerous situation. He had watched confidently as the boy cut in front of the little señora and grabbed her purse. He saw her stiffen with surprise, and the boy's roguish face staring back at her. Almost as if he were in the small body he had shared the wild surge of triumph; then, as the boy collided with the tall, graying man, he experienced the jarring impact, the bewilderment, even breathless fright.

He had been so certain of the perfection of his own plotting that he couldn't fully realize what had happened. He sat frozen where he was watching the crowd gather, his mind, like a camera, without selection recording everything around him; the dry, withered appearance of the grass, the ornate metal scrolls on the backs of the benches which were suddenly emptied as the people rushed toward the screaming boy.

The initial touch of fear came when the black car pulled to the curb with the inspector staring out of the rear window; but before the fear could crystallize, the car pulled away again. It was the sight of the policeman elbowing his way through the crowd that really warned Luis to be frightened. As clearly as though she were sitting beside him, he could hear his mother's voice saying, "There will be trouble with the police"; and he knew he must leave immediately before the boy could identify him. Hastily he folded his newspaper, and remembering that the crumpled white bag could be evidence, thrust it into his pocket. The gumdrops he had used to entice the boys were gone, leaving only specks of sugar that were gritty against his hand. He looked around cautiously for the black car, but it was gone.

As quickly as he dared, he crossed the street. It was noon. There was little traffic, few shoppers. Although he felt conspicuous as he started down one of the narrow, shaded streets that led from the square, no one noticed him. The shopkeepers drawn out from the coolness of the stores onto the heat of the sidewalk, the few pedestrians who were in the area were all watching the Plaza.

Not until he was several blocks away did his fright begin to subside, but he still had the terrifying illusion that the police were after him. He expected to hear the sound of footsteps running behind him, braced himself against a warning shout. But nothing happened and finally his mind settled slowly into dull apprehension. He wondered whether the boy would describe him and if his description could be recognized. He sorted through the faces on the Plaza, trying to decide whether anyone there might have known him.

Aimlessly he wandered the streets trying to assess the

97

extent of his danger, at first not thinking clearly, finally marshaling his thoughts so that he could examine them logically. After all, what could the boy say? He didn't know Luis. The description? "Medium build . . . not old . . . wearing brown slacks and a white shirt." That could fit almost anyone. And what would happen when the police looked for him? Nothing! Someone else would be sitting on the bench he had occupied. The paper bag, the newspaper, every sign of him would be gone. The police would simply believe that the boy had been lying.

Once he was calm enough to review the evidence objectively, Luis was reassured that his alarm was groundless. While he was still confused and frightened he had thought briefly of going to the gas station, and now he found that unconsciously he had headed in that direction. Even if he were not out of danger, Luis reasoned, following the familiar pattern of his days offered the surest protection against suspicion. Of course there was no danger. His conflict with the police had been purely imaginary. Nevertheless, whatever he told himself, Luis remained convinced that he had had a narrow escape.

He determined to give up his pursuit of the emerald. Its green beauty, its fantastic value were a temptation, but his deep, unreasoning fear of the police warned him that there was no safe way to recover it. He had too much to lose to take unnecessary risks.

"After all," he reflected, "even without the emerald, things are not so bad. I can wait. I am young, attractive to women. Something will turn up. I earn enough to live, the tourists pay me well." His logic, based on an acceptance of failure, comforted him.

On the sun-drenched highway to the station he passed some Indians who were resting beside the road, squatting on the ground like tired beasts of burden. He noticed the string of shacks that extended back toward the hills, with dirty children playing in the flowerless yards. His own poverty-stricken childhood was there before him, and automatically he looked at his gold wristwatch, not seeing the time, just making an automatic comparison with his present comforts.

He thought of his large, cool room, the handsome coat, finer than any he had ever seen in the shops of San Luis. He thought of the tips he would earn in the afternoon and the expensive dinner they would buy. He thought of Carmelita's soft body and the warm passion of her velvety eyes. It had been a long time since Luis had enumerated the many good things life offered to him, and when again he considered gambling with danger for the emerald, he decided once more that he had too much to lose.

By the time he reached the gas station, he was cheerfully reconciled to returning to the uneventful security that being a guide offered him. He walked up to the pumps, waiting for the arrival of the earliest tourists. There was the usual activity. Trucks and an occasional passenger car kept pulling in for gas. The small boys cleaned the windshields with their energetic, useless industry and between jobs compared their hoard of pesos. The only attendant was working underneath the hoist. The thin, dour station manager was kept busy by a succession of cars, yet it seemed to Luis that he was eyeing him peculiarly as if he had something unpleasant to say and was only waiting for an opportunity to say it.

At last, at one of the rare intervals when the station was completely empty, while the small boys were huddling in the shade beside the building and the attendant was still working under the car, the manager approached and asked Luis point-blank, "What do the police want with you?"

The question frightened uis. "Were they here again today?"

"No, yesterday. The sergeant came for you."

"Oh, that!" Luis' relief was obvious. "They wanted to

99

know something about the Indian village. I was there yesterday morning."

The manager chewed a toothpick speculatively. "I don't want the police here. After they took you away some others came. They searched the station. If you're mixed up with them I don't want you hanging around."

Without the gas station the bulk of Luis' income would be lost. Like a poor swimmer who has gone beyond his depth, Luis fought the beginnings of panic. Unconvincingly he protested, "I'm not mixed up with them, I tell you! They asked me about the Indians."

The manager didn't answer, but Luis could see that he was mulling it over, weighing the few pesos he received from Luis against involvement with the police. In another minute Luis was certain he would be told to leave.

Before any decision could be made, however, a low, red sports car pulled up to the pump. It was an expensive English import with long, sweeping fenders, leather seats, discreet touches of chrome and the familiar green *turista* sticker on the windshield. The handsome man in his early forties who climbed out had the well-groomed casual appearance that comes only with wealth. The woman in the car rested her head against the leather seat as though she were very tired.

Assuming his right to be there, Luis eagerly approached the tourist, but under his outward assurance he was aware that the manager continued to watch him doubtfully. With grave politeness he translated the tourists' instructions about servicing the car, making them sound more exacting than they really were, hoping that the manager would be reminded of Luis' value to the station as an interpreter.

"We'd like to get to Mexico City tonight," the driver was saying. "Can we make it?"

"It's too far." Luis shook his head. "You'd never get there before midnight. And there are mountains to cross."

The woman in the car turned around and said in a soft, impatient voice, "Let's go as far as we can anyway, Chuck." She was the most beautiful woman Luis had ever seen, her skin pale and smooth as a camellia petal, her mouth full, red and sensual, her eyes mist-colored, fringed by thick, dark lashes. There was something arrogant, challenging in her manner that enhanced her beauty and reminded Luis, without apparent connection, of the emerald.

"We'll go on," the man agreed, dismissing Luis with a small tip and turning to talk to the woman as though the guide were no longer there.

The manager was in the office getting change for the gasoline. In a few minutes he would return; the tourists would leave and the uncomfortable conversation would be resumed. Although it was much too early for the heaviest flow of tourist traffic, Luis dared not stay. He had scarcely enough money in his pocket to buy a meal, yet he could not afford to force a decision. If he lost his place at the gas station, there would no longer be any security for him. Where would he meet the tourists? How would he earn his hotel commissions? Before the manager could return, Luis left the station and started back along the dusty shoulder of the road toward town.

The discomforts which he had not noticed on the way out became all-encompassing. The heat burned his shoulders through the thin shirt. Small pebbles crept into his shoes and bored against the soles of his feet. He was frightened again, too, not by anything tangible like the police, but by something that had neither shape nor form, the threatened loss of his livelihood. He was at the mercy of the station manager and that offered very little hope indeed.

Perhaps it was reaction to his torn and frustrating day, but suddenly Luis became bitterly, irrationally angry. Just as he had when he stole the car, he seethed with rebellious resentment against circumstance. Mentally he struck out at forces over which he had no control, refusing to accept them. He cursed the Indian for selling him the jewel. He cursed the boy for not getting it back. He cursed the police for alarming the station manager. He cursed himself for his own timidity and decided he was, after all, going to get the jewel. He hoped he would not have to harm the little señora, but the emerald was his and he intended to have it. He would try to avoid violence, but if there were no alternative . . .

Luis thought grimly, "If it is necessary, I will do it." But what he would do, or how he would do it, he did not know. He only knew that he would not meekly be pushed into poverty.

The red sports car raced past him insolently trailing a cloud of dust, and, from the shoulder of the highway, Luis glared after it, resentment against the conditions of his own life briefly refocused against the rich and favored —the *turistas*, who did not dangle, precariously, as he did, above the brink of poverty. In their sleek, high-powered cars the North Americans could come and go as they pleased. Even the little señora. In the morning she could pile her luggage into the white convertible and leave San Luis, taking with her the handbag, the jewel and his own hopes of freedom and wealth. It made Luis realize that time was running out for him and added urgency to his desperation. He began to hurry toward San Luis thinking, anxiously, that perhaps only a few hours remained before the emerald would be beyond his reach forever.

When he reached the city proper he was surprised to find that the siesta was not yet over. The torpor of sleep lay everywhere. The shops were shuttered against the severe heat. The labyrinth of streets was almost empty. So much had happened that Luis found it difficult to realize that it was still this early in the afternoon. Some of

102

his urgency faded. There was time to think, time to plan; for not in his most reckless imaginings would Luis have considered acting in the harsh brightness of day.

His own street, the building in which he lived drowsed in the same silence as the others around it. The courtyard, usually crowded with chattering women, contained only one tangle-haired little girl who stared at his passing with wide, sleepy eyes. He climbed the steps to his room, grateful for its coolness, realizing that he was tired, that his thoughts were confused.

He slid out of his burning shoes and stretched out on the bed, trying to relax his body and calm his mind into some kind of order.

"The advantage lies with me," he reasoned. "I know where the jewel is. I can easily enter the Villa grounds and, after last night, I know I can easily get out." Idly he wondered why Carmelita had always insisted that he leave before Uncle Pedro locked the gate. "It's so simple to get out," he mused, returning to his main objective. "I know the little señora's room, the arrangement of the furniture, the closet that holds her clothes. It would be easy to hide there."

But Luis was uncertain. The señora would see him and she was sure to scream. Already his native caution was reasserting itself. What good would the jewel do him if he were taken by the police?

Restlessly he got off the bed and started to pace the room in noiseless stockinged feet. His fear of exposure blotted out everything else. He was aware of his mind's inertia, his inability to push past the wall of conditioning. Besides, he was distracted by the needs of his body. He remembered that he had eaten nothing all day and, realizing it, his hunger immediately became more important than anything else.

He shook the dry coffeepot, searched for a piece of

bread, and found, instead, some small apples with tough, shriveled skins. He started to peel one with his pocket knife, then stopped, staring with fascination at the thin, shining blade. He pushed the blade back into its holder, snapped the release button and watched it pop out again.

Inadvertently he again pictured the señora's room, this time her bathroom, all shining tile, smelling faintly of lavender, and the window that looked out into the woods behind the Villa. The window! It had been open! He was sure of it!

How simple it all really was, he decided. He would cut the screen of the bathroom window and hide in the shelter of the trees. After the little señora was asleep, he would quietly, very quietly, crawl through the window, find her purse and get his jewel. He would move soundlessly and she would not awaken.

But what would he do if she did awaken? The dangerous question intruded above and below his planning.

"She won't even turn over," he assured himself. "But if she does . . ." He looked at the shining blade of the knife, ran his finger over the dull edge, put aside the half-peeled apple and searched through the drawer for a small, square whetstone.

Outside, a woman's high-pitched, worried voice abruptly cut the heavy silence. "Rita! Rita! Where are you?"

And the little girl in the courtyard answered, "Here, Mamá."

As if a spigot had been opened the street sounds began to flow again, the gradually ascending pitch of the traffic, the shouts of the peddlers, the barking dogs, the chatter of voices. It was three o'clock. The siesta was over.

Inside his room Luis thought of the little señora and carefully, methodically, sharpened his knife.

fifteen

FROM the sun-baked steps of the cathedral it appeared to Jessie as if the siesta had interrupted nothing. The endless procession was crossing and crisscrossing the Plaza. The same children, it seemed, were chasing the same dogs around the fountain. The snow-cone vendor was doing a brisk business at his carnival-colored stand. The heat, the glare, the dust were all equally intense.

"It's as hot as it was at noon," Jessie commented, trying to adjust to the noise and confusion after the quiet intimacy of the church.

"Not as hot, hotter." Burt smiled and helped her down the steep steps. His smile dispelled the brief awkwardness that had sprung up between them.

Something about the shadowed refuge of the church had, unexpectedly, stripped away the artifices of adulthood and for a brief hour had drawn them together with the unreasoning closeness of children. The hundreds of flickering votive candles, perhaps, or the crippled woman who knelt at the foot of a garishly ornamented Virgin had led Burt to talk of his wife's death. He told how the deforming power of her illness had corroded them both, until, at the end, he had almost wanted Marilyn to die. When it was over, he said, he had been rootless, guilty, unable to find any life outside his work.

"Of course," he concluded, "sooner or later we all have to come to terms with the past and face the future."

Although he spoke quietly, dispassionately, of something that had happened long ago, his tragedy was so vivid to Jessie that, in comparison, her own problems seemed self-created, almost trivial.

"Yesterday," she said softly, "I thought I couldn't live without Dan. Now, hearing about Marilyn, I wonder if I ever did live with him."

Afterward, in the sharp glare of the sunlight, she was almost embarrassed by her revealing communication, but Burt seemed instantly to forget the mood of the church as though it, too, were part of the siesta.

"At three o'clock," he said, "a master alarm goes off, and everyone, all over Mexico, rushes into the streets."

And, in fact, as Jessie drove back to the Villa, she did find the narrow streets more crowded. All the tiny shops had reopened, people were clustered around the open stalls of fruit and meat, overflowing the narrow sidewalks onto the cobblestoned road and joining with the carts and bicycles in obstructing traffic.

"Everything is foreign, so different," she said.

"I don't know," Burt said casually. "It's about the same as Los Angeles' Olivera Street. . . . If there still is an Olivera Street."

"There is—but look at that! That's something you'll never see on Olivera Street."

An old Indian on a burro crossed the intersection in front of them. He was wearing a huge palm-frond hat that obscured his features, but the bony legs that reached almost to the ground on either side of his tiny animal gave the impression that he was very skinny.

Although Burt took the Indian's presence for granted, to Jessie it was an anachronism here in an age of automobiles and electricity.

"It's like an overlapping of time," she protested. "To stop for a man on a donkey."

Because his very existence seemed to be so incongruous

106

he had no more reality for her than an illustration out of a storybook. His world was so many centuries removed from the world in which she lived that it would never have occurred to Jessie that his life could even remotely impinge on her own.

The old Indian followed the Calle Madero until he found a small, unpretentious jewelry store. There he tied his burro to a post, went in, and hesitantly handed the jeweler a ring.

Even though the shopkeeper had never handled a ring of this quality before, it was oddly familiar. There was no emerald in the mounting but, without it, the platinum band with the row of diamonds around the setting exactly matched a description that had been circulated by the police. Remembering the warning that a ring like this one was evidence in a murder case, the jeweler immediately called the authorities.

According to the police blotter, at precisely four o'clock, on October tenth, the Indian was arrested.

Although this event was vital to his case, Inspector Menendes had not been notified. He was in his hot, airless office behind the police station filling out a complicated form from the Randalls' insurance company and wishing that he were at home in the coolness of the courtyard watching María play near the fountain.

The clock was ticking away the minutes of what had been a thoroughly annoying day. First there had been the irritation of the reporters, then the interfering call from Mexico City, and finally the lunch with the United States consul which had ended on a note of frigid politeness. Charles Morton had asked searching questions that the inspector could not answer without exposing the direction of his investigation. His evasions had been obvious and Charles had terminated them by saying:

"The Randalls, you know, were very rich and influential. Both of our governments consider the solution of their murder as something of the greatest importance."

"I'm well aware of that," the inspector had answered hostilely. "And if I can pursue the case in my own way I'll find the murderer."

But even as he said it, he wasn't so sure. If the Indians were prematurely alarmed, he would never find the murderer, and with everyone pressuring him for particulars, how long could he keep the spotlight from them?

The afternoon continued in the same annoying pattern. On his desk was a report covering the incident on the Plaza. It, too, involved a tourist, just at a time when he could least afford more unfavorable publicity. A Mrs. Jessie Prewitt, stopping at the Villa Serena, was crossing the Plaza when her purse was stolen. The purse had been recovered and returned to her, but the culprit eluded the police. Well, at least, there was some consolation in the fact that she had her property back; if nothing were missing, there would probably be no repercussions.

He put the report aside and started to work on the official forms required for the shipment of the Randalls' remains when the phone rang. The local radio station wanted to know whether there were any late developments that should be included in the hourly broadcast. That call was followed immediately by another from a crime reporter who wanted permission to take pictures of the bodies. He was so very persistent that the inspector finally disconnected him in the middle of a sentence. The irritation which had been bubbling close to the surface all day overflowed. He picked up the receiver and snapped at the operator, "No more calls. No matter who it is, I'm not in."

And that was why, when the jeweler phoned, the message did not reach him. Instead, the lieutenant in charge took the call and, knowing that there was a reward for the ring, it was he who went out to bring in the criminal.

The old Indian was confused. He couldn't understand what the police wanted with him or what they were saying when they asked about the missing stone from the ring. His few words of Spanish escaped him and, while they were pushing him toward the police van, he kept protesting loudly in Nahuatl that he couldn't go with them, that he couldn't leave his donkey.

Lieutenant Jiminez, small, violent, quick-tempered, became enraged at the Indian's behavior. Certain that the old man had secreted the jewel, that he was only feigning ignorance of Spanish and that he was now trying to escape, the lieutenant used language that he was positive the crafty thief would understand. He grabbed the old man roughly by his loose shirt, pummeled him with his fists, asking with every blow about the emerald. Finally, in disgust, he threw the Indian into the van to crouch on the floor still protesting about his burro.

By the time they reached the police station, the Indian had cloaked himself in the same sullen silence that his ancestors had used as a protection against their oppressors Not even the interpreter could get anything out of him, for, although he spoke the Aztec tongue, he was wearing the uniform of the enemy and the Indian identified him with them. When they threatened him, he said nothing. When they beat him, he bowed under the blows, whimpering softly like a child in pain.

Finally because he could get nothing out of the stubborn old fool, and because, without the jewel, the reward would escape him anyway, the lieutenant gave the useless ring to Sergeant Roberto, and only then did he call the inspector.

The inspector, just locking his desk when the phone rang, picked up the receiver, braced for another unpleasant call. He was surprised when the lieutenant said, "We've found your murderer." Before Menendes had a chance to doubt it, the lieutenant continued, "We caught him trying to sell the ring."

"Who is he?" the inspector asked, knowing in advance the importance of the answer.

"An Indian, an old one."

Without waiting for him to finish, the inspector interrupted. "I'll be right over."

The lieutenant and Sergeant Roberto were waiting for him at the police desk. Without speaking the sergeant handed him the ring, and he held it for a moment examining the cold shimmer of the diamonds on the mounting and trying to rise above a wave of anger that washed over him.

When he spoke his voice was ominously controlled. "Why wasn't I notified?"

It was the sergeant who answered as though the question had been addressed directly to him. "I didn't know anything about it, sir. I saw them bring the Indian in, but no one told me why he was arrested."

The lieutenant arrogantly cut into his explanation. "The sergeant was on the phone. We had orders you weren't to be disturbed. So I went after the man myself. We interrogated him, but got nowhere."

Holding the ring between his massive thumb and forefinger so that the hole in the mounting was evident to them all, the inspector said dryly, "You mean you couldn't get him to tell you where the jewel was."

The lieutenant flushed uneasily. "We couldn't get him to tell us anything."

It wasn't because they hadn't tried, the inspector decided grimly, when he saw the Indian huddled like a bundle of old clothes on the bunk. Brutality of any sort sickened him. He considered it the final resort of stupidity, and when it was employed by the police, he was ashamed to be numbered among them. Now, looking at the man's bruised face, he didn't think about his being the murderer or about the empty ring; he thought only that he would report the lieutenant, that, if possible, he would have him suspended from the force.

He spoke gently, first in Spanish, then, when the old man didn't answer, in Nahuatl. "Don't be afraid, Uncle. I only want to help."

Perhaps it was because the large man in the dark suit was an Indian like himself; perhaps it was only because the old man so badly needed a friend, but he began to talk in a cracked, hoarse voice. He told the inspector how the police had arrested him at the jewelry store and about his burro who was still waiting there in this unfriendly city without anyone to care for him.

"I will send someone for your burro, Uncle. We will find a place for him to sleep."

The old man was obviously relieved. Apparently his own predicament seemed less serious to him than the comfort of his animal. Had he been a mestizo or European, the inspector would have been certain of the man's innocence; but, because he was an Indian it could merely mean that he did not believe that killing and robbing foreigners was a punishable crime.

"I will take care of your burro, but first you must tell me about the ring."

The old man hesitated as if wondering where to begin; then, in the manner of the old storytellers, he described his village, pinpointing its exact location by familiar landmarks, the arroyo that led to it, the stunted grove of ancient trees, the crumbling idol of one of the old gods. "We are very poor in my village," he said. "And I am very poor as my father was poor before me. I have no son, only my grandson. It is the time now to pick corn, but the corn is not good. I thought . . . it could not hurt to leave some grain for the old god, perhaps he could make the harvest better. I left the grain and when I came again, the grain was gone, only the ring was there."

The missing grain, the ring left in exchange. It was like a fantasy, an imaginative lie created by a child. The inspector listened carefully, trying to extract whatever truth lay in it, mentally calculating the distance from the old man's village to the spot at which the Randalls were killed. Not over seven miles, an easy trip for a man with a donkey.

Still, could this be the murderer? Surely someone capable of planning a crime so carefully, of stealing only money and jewelry would be too worldly to offer such an unsophisticated explanation. . . . Unless he were very, very crafty . . . unless he only pretended to be simple. The inspector searched the old man's face for traces of slyness, but the light was already growing dim and he could no longer see the man clearly.

The ring in his hand reminded him that this was the clue he had been looking for, the one that would lead him to the murderer and he pressed ahead, trying to take the Indian unawares.

"What about the tourists?" he asked matter-of-factly as though they both knew the tourists were involved. "Were they at the shrine?"

The old man didn't take the bait. "Tourists, what tourists?" Was his voice wary, or just perplexed?

"And the stone, the one that belongs in the ring. Where is that?" the inspector persisted.

"There was no stone. My grandson was with me, he'll tell you."

"We'll question your grandson," the inspector said and immediately regretted the words. They sounded unnaturally harsh and threatening. He tried to soften them by adding, "If what you say is true, you can return to your people."

112

But it was too late. He had revealed himself as a policeman, one of the enemy, and the old man had already retreated into his stubborn silence.

When the inspector asked with apparent irrelevance, "Tell me, Uncle, do you own a rifle?" he might have been speaking to an empty cell. He knew then that, like the others, he had failed.

He unlocked the door and stepped out into the corridor, stopping only long enough to say, "I will care for your burro and tomorrow, after I have been to the village, we will talk again."

His tone was soft, but he was experiencing the same impatience that the lieutenant or Sergeant Roberto would have felt. He was thoroughly annoyed by the old Indian, and it was tempting to build a case against him. There was the ring, the ridiculous story. . . . How could the ring show up seven miles from the scene of the crime?

He walked out into the station. The huge, barnlike doors were open to receive the first, cool evening breezes; the night man was already there, reading his magazine. Both the lieutenant and the sergeant were waiting for him at the police desk, the lieutenant's eyes gleaming with avarice, the sergeant's with curiosity.

"Well, did he confess?" the lieutenant asked. "Did you tell you where the jewel is?"

"He confessed nothing. In fact," he added more to humble the lieutenant than for any other reason, "I'm not even sure he's the murderer." As he said it he knew that it was true. A residue of doubt remained, no larger, perhaps, than the hole in the mounting, but it was there. "Sergeant, send someone after the Indian's burro. Have it stabled with the police horses."

He saw the contemptuous raising of the lieutenant's eyebrow and the doubt that touched the sergeant's face

113

and knew that they believed that he was pampering the Indian.

"Even an Indian," he said acidly, "is entitled to protection under the law. We know that he has the ring and that it's possible he's the murderer—but it's up to us to prove it. It could be, you know, that he found the ring or that it was given to him by someone else."

He turned to Sergeant Roberto. "Tomorrow morning we'll go to the old man's village. This time I'm coming with you. Let's get an early start."

Automatically he placed his finger over the hole in the mounting, and, feeling the uneven position of the prongs, knew that the jewel had been forcibly removed. With the sixth sense of a good detective, he realized that this was an important detail, but for the moment he was unable to relate its importance to the rest of the case.

"Lieutenant," he said, "I'm leaving it to you to warn the moneylenders, jewelry stores, silversmiths, anyone who makes jewelry, that we are looking for a stone, an emerald, unusually large, almost square."

He sounded more decisive than he felt. Through the open doors he could see the lamps in front of the police station already glowing dimly in the cool gray light, the faded, almost colorless pallor of the sky. In another hour it would be dark. He felt unsure of his own reasoning, his own ability. Like the day itself the case seemed to be slipping away from him.

sixteen/

THE LIGHT was fading over the Villa, too. It fell on Jessie's book, reminding her that it was time to dress for the party. She had been sitting there without reading, thinking of the hour in the cathedral and the strange way in which new horizons of sensitivity and understanding were opening for her. In the room behind her, shadows had already gathered. Outside her window the details of the garden and the wall surrounding it were rapidly blurring into a monotone of gray. The scene had a misty, luminous beauty that she tried to capture and weave into the serape of impressions that she would take with her from San Luis.

Not that she wanted to leave San Luis, but, as Burt said, sooner or later she would have to come to terms with the past and face the future. Distance, a rebirth of her ability to think more objectively, made her question the wisdom of her headlong flight. It had solved nothing and it could solve nothing. It was impossible to escape forever from the things that pained her; ultimately they must be faced.

"I'll have to go back," she said aloud, her mind reluctantly traveling the routes back to the States.

There was the road over which she had come, and the central one through Eagle Pass—or maybe she could take that other highway, the long one Burt had told her about, west to Morelia and Guadalajara, Mazatlán and, finally, north to Nogales.

"It's not as fast as the highway from Monterrey," he had said. "It winds and twists and every year parts of it are washed out by flood—but it's always passable and it gives you a real idea of the grandeur and contrasts of Mexico."

He had described the huge, forested mountains, the hot plains where iguanas, looking like miniature prehistoric monsters, can sometimes be seen racing across the pavement; the tropical growth as the road nears the coast; and the beautiful blue waters of the Gulf of California.

"I'd like to take that trip," Jessie had said at lunch, not seriously considering the possibility.

But now, thinking about it again, she knew that she wanted to return that way, that she could not bear to travel back again through Monterrey. The emptiness of the terrain had become intertwined in her mind with the emptiness of her relationship with Dan. For some obscure, unanalyzed reason, she felt that by taking a different, more promising road, the future, too, would be different.

"It will probably turn out the same in the end," she mused, smiling at her own wishful imaginings, "but at least the scenery along the way will be interesting."

Not certain that she could afford the longer trip, she dumped the contents of her purse on the bed and counted the remaining traveler's checks. There were fewer than she expected; and estimating the miles and the cost, she was still uncertain. Then she noticed the tobacco pouch and recalled the guide who had sold it to her. His face was indistinct. All she could remember was his urgent voice, the film of sweat on his forehead, the absurdly warm coat, the purple stones that lay in his hand. She picked up the pouch to look inside, and touching it reminded her again of the drive from Monterrey.

"Whatever happens I have to go back a different way,"

she decided suddenly, not really seeing the amethyst that had torn through the tissue paper and that she picked up and held to the light, but thinking, without logical sequence, of the Randalls. They, too, had driven along that desolate highway. On either side of them had been the same yellow hills and the unbroken azure of the sky. Malignant eyes that might have been watching for her peered out beyond the curve, waiting . . . waiting. . . .

A nebulous fantasy that had been slowly building at the back of Jessie's mind became articulate. "If I had been a day earlier, it would not have been the Randalls who were murdered. My body, my car would have been found smashed against the rocks."

The macabre idea was distressingly real. She put the purple stone back into the pouch with the others and dropped it into her purse, piling traveler's checks, compact, entrance papers and wallet all back on top of it, eager to get it out of her sight as if it were responsible for her eerie thought. Once it was hidden she wondered what had possessed her the moment before and why she had bought the stones to start with.

Quickly, refusing to think any more about them or the roads or of the strange lottery of death that connected her with the Randalls, she started to change her clothes for the party, wondering what a Mexican birthday party could be like and if they would really have fireworks.

Emily and Rose were going, she had learned, Ralph Burton and a couple named "Groom." "You remember them," Ruth Alexander had said when she reminded Jessie of the invitation. "They sat at my table last night. Becky's the large, very pretty girl; Tom's slight, a little bald. Immediately after the cocktail hour we'll meet at the parking lot."

Rather than be late Jessie left her room a few minutes early and hurried through the black-and-silver night, grateful for the fresh, peppery breezes that had blown away the warmth of the day. She followed the dramatic spotlights thrown by the lanterns, up the stone steps of the garden, past Uncle Pedro who sat on a wooden box guarding the gate and into the lot where the cars huddled in conspiratorial darkness.

It was so quiet there that she thought that she was the first to arrive, but except for Rose and Emily the others were already waiting, talking in the subdued voices that night seems to demand.

"You look lovely, Jessie," Burt said as she joined them. "Ethereal and wispy. In fact, I can hardly see you. By the way have you met the Grooms?"

Before Jessie could answer, Emily was there, breathlessly complaining, "I've lost Rose. She stopped to talk to the gatekeeper, and with my Spanish, I couldn't get a barb in edgewise."

"We're in no hurry. She'll be along," Ruth Alexander said calmly. "Which car will we take?"

Jessie suggested that Burt drive all of them over in her convertible, but after she had pressed in close beside him to allow room for the others, Ruth Alexander objected that it would be too crowded.

"I'll go ahead with Becky and Tom. We'll meet you there."

While they waited for Rose, Burt turned toward the back seat to talk to Emily, casually placing his arm around Jessie's shoulder. She was conscious of his nearness and that there was now room to move away, but she liked the dry, warm touch of his hand, the soap-clean smell about him that matched his appearance. She wanted to lay her head against his chest as she used to do with Dan. Instead she sat rigidly upright, not wishing to encourage him, yet reluctant to end the comforting physical contact. At last he said, "Here's Rose," and took his arm away.

Aware that her stiffness might have rebuffed him, Jessie would have liked to say something that would re-create an intimacy between them, but no words would come except the awkward ones to Rose, "We've been waiting for you."

And Emily added with exasperation, "I don't know why you can't ever be on time."

"I just stopped for a moment to talk with the gate-keeper and I couldn't get away. He's not happy."

"I know," Burt said, starting the car and groping blindly out of the parking lot with the dimmed headlights customary in Mexico. "His nose is out of joint because he won't get to see the fireworks."

"How did you know—about the gatekeeper I mean?" Rose asked.

"Well you're not the only one who speaks Spanish, Rose. I'm an old pro myself."

"If he's told you about his niece, I've run out of gossip."

"You mean the pretty one who's been sneaking out behind the barn with that good-looking boy who works in the lounge? Yes, he told me about her, too, and the lucky man who's been courting her. I understand it's our local guide."

"The guide?" Jessie asked. "Is there only one?"

"Yes," Rose answered. "A very sleek, smooth young man. Do you know him?"

"No, not really. Yesterday, at the gas station, he sold me some amethysts. I was looking at them tonight wondering what in the world to do with them. They're just loose stones and I suppose I should throw them away but my thrifty Scotch soul won't let me. After all I did give fifty pesos for them."

"If they're any good at all fifty pesos is a bargain," Emily said. "For a dollar or two you can have them made

119

into a pair of earrings or a bracelet. They'll make a wonderful, inexpensive gift. I'm part Scotch myself and I wouldn't throw them away."

"Where would I take them?"

"There are dozens of silversmiths. The cheapest place I know of is Aguinaldo's," Rose suggested. "It's on the same street as the Cathedral, two blocks south. You can't miss it. From the outside it looks like a junk shop. They sell just about everything there, and make and repair jewelry, too."

Jessie was pleased to have found a use for the stones. "Tomorrow," she said excitedly, "I'll take them over there. I think I'd like to have a silver bracelet. I've never had one. Burt," she added impulsively taking his arm, "would you go with me and help pick out a design?"

Burt looked down at her and said with teasing affection, "Well, selecting jewelry is not really my specialty, but if it will help any I'll coach from the sidelines." He turned up the headlights and they shone on a long line of cars on the street ahead. "Here we are. Now all I have to do is find a parking spot."

They were in front of a huge, discreetly lighted house that was set far back from the road. They could hear the beat of drums and the rattle of maracas that rose and fell with the intermittent breeze.

It was the first time Jessie had ever been to a party without Dan and she felt a twinge of guilt at her surge of happy excitement. But it was only momentary, drowned by the rhythmic beat of the music, the sound of distant laughter, the pressure of Burt's hand as he helped her out of the car, and the clear, scented promise of the night.

seventeen

As HE USUALLY did, Luis arrived at the Villa while the tourists were at dinner. It was a dangerously bright and cloudless night, but at this hour there was little chance of meeting anyone in either the parking lot or the garden.

Long ago Uncle Pedro had warned him against attracting attention to his evening visits. "I know it's all right," the gatekeeper had said, "but the Señora Alexander? Who knows how North Americans think?"

Carmelita too had insisted on secrecy. She would meet him outside the kitchen door after dinner was over; together they would walk to the ancient tree on which the merchant had hanged himself, and there they would sit, shielded from curious eyes by the festooned moss and superstition that clung to it. When Luis, nervous under the evil tree, had jokingly accused her of hiding from another lover among the servants, Carmelita had flashed with instant anger.

"A lover, yes indeed I have a lover—Uncle Pedro. At his age where would he find another job? One that is so easy and pays so well? If you don't like it, don't come at all!"

Luis had sulked for several days before he had returned on her terms, humiliated by his defeat, yet drawn by the passionate promise of her velvet eyes, the ripeness of her lips, the sinuous smoothness of her body.

Now, through a queer twist of destiny, his very defeat worked out to his advantage. The secret visits made both Carmelita and the gatekeeper his unwitting allies. If anything went wrong, they would be forced to protect him. Certainly they could not admit that, without permission, he had been given unquestioned access to the Villa.

Boldly he crossed the dark, walled pit of the parking lot and stepped out into the molten silver moonlight that flowed through the open gate. His intentions, honed to the razor sharpness of his knife, were sheathed behind a pleasant smile.

To the gatekeeper Luis looked as he always did—handsome and prosperous in his expensive tan coat. Again he thought what a fine husband the guide would make for Carmelita. If the girl would only come to her senses! He had talked to her, scolded her, but it was like trying to stop a river from flowing. She flashed those big eyes of hers at every handsome man and twitched her busy bottom. One of these days she would end up in real trouble. Tonight . . . who knew what she would do without Uncle Pedro to watch her? The brief smile that had animated his face when he first saw Luis died, and he sighed dejectedly.

"What's the matter, Uncle Pedro?" Luis asked cheerfully. "You're not yourself tonight."

"They've all gone," the gatekeeper said, as though from those few, glum words Luis would know what he was talking about.

"Who's gone?"

"Carmelita and the others. They've gone to see the fireworks. You know, at Ramón Morales' house. Only Uncle Pedro has to stay. 'Someone must watch the gate,' she said." His voice mimicked Ruth Alexander's flat Midwestern accent.

"Don't feel bad, Uncle Pedro. You've seen fireworks before, and you will again." He offered the gatekeeper a cigarette and patted him lightly on the shoulder. "Anyway," he improvised swiftly, "I didn't come only to see Carmelita. The Señora Alexander still owes me a *mordida* for sending the little *turista*."

"She's gone too," the gatekeeper said, shaking his head.

Could it be that the woman had already left San Luis, that the jewel was already beyond his reach? He heard the alarm in his own voice. "Who's gone? The little señora?"

"Both of them. Only today's *turistas* are here. All the others have gone with Señora Alexander to the party!"

So the woman had not escaped him! Luis' relief was so complete and immediate that he did not realize, at first, that he had used up his only reasonable excuses for entering the Villa grounds.

"How long have they been gone?"

"You just missed them!"

After waiting through the leaden setting of the sun, the lingering golden afterglow, fearful of being too early, he had arrived too late. Realization was a bitter anticlimax. His mind cautioned him against arousing suspicion, yet his determination drove him to persist.

"Perhaps I'll wait for Carmelita."

"It's useless, *amigo*. They will come back late and all together. No, it's better to go yourself and watch the fireworks. They will be wonderful. Señor Morales is very rich."

There was no course open to Luis but to admit defeat and leave. "If I had only come earlier," he thought. "I would be in there now, hiding safely behind the Villa."

Tormented by "if's," he started back to town. He could almost imagine that the bad luck which had plagued him for the past few days was padding after him through the night-shrouded streets. He tried to tell him-

123

self that all was not lost, but, with the way his luck had been running, the little *turista* would, without a doubt, leave in the morning—and there was nothing he could do to stop her.

Unwilling to be alone with his despondent thoughts, he turned into the first *cantina*. At the crowded bar he found a place near the end where a large, flabby man was talking to the barmaid.

"I always come back, Rosa," the man was saying. "Sooner or later you know I always come back."

On the other side of him someone was talking about the National Lottery, certain that it was fixed because he had never won. At a table beside the bar four men were playing a fast, loud game of cards. The noise, the congenial atmosphere, the warmth of tequila in his stomach restored some of Luis' optimism. Granted, his luck had been bad, but as with all luck, it would have to change. Perhaps, after all, the little señora would not leave in the morning.

The place was growing increasingly crowded. A stout, jolly man whom everyone greeted familiarly as "Pepe" bought drinks for the bar. He came over to the man who was beside Luis.

"I thought you were supposed to pull out this morning, Gonzales."

"I was. I got about five miles north and blew the left rear."

"Couldn't you buy another tire?"

"In San Luis? Who're you kidding? They show you pictures of tires and order them from the capital. They sent it in on the four o'clock bus. It was too late then to leave." He finished his beer and put the glass down on the bar with a gesture of disgust.

Leaning over to pick it up, her naked breasts showing provocatively under the low-cut blouse, the barmaid winked across at Luis. "Don't you believe him, Pepe. He didn't blow a tire at all. He drove a nail into it."

124

Pepe laughed. "Who could blame him, Rosa? Here, bring us another drink."

During their conversation Luis had grown increasingly excited. It was as though fate itself had intervened to help him.

"Excuse me, Señores," he interrupted. "I couldn't help overhearing. Is it really so tough to get tires in San Luis?"

Gonzales answered. "If you take an odd size or need more than one," he shrugged. "San Luis is no different from other places. It's the same all over. I usually carry an extra spare—just for insurance. Did you need a tire?"

"No," Luis said. "A friend of mine does."

He finished his drink quickly and got up. The barmaid, just bringing the beer for the men beside him, smiled at him enticingly, and at any other time Luis would have noticed how white and even her teeth were, the swinging invitation of her hips.

"You leaving, Señor?" She really sounded disappointed. "Later we'll have guitar music and Pepe will sing."

"I have to go," Luis said. "Maybe I'll be back," and because the liquor made the remark seem to be a clever one, he added, "I'm going to take out some insurance."

Outside in the cool, sobering air, away from the comradeship of the bar, Luis regretted the reckless remark; but, because his confidence in himself and in his future had been thoroughly restored, he was unable to worry about it. He was sure, now, that nothing could harm him, that his luck had finally changed. After all, what could it be but good fortune that had led him to that particular *cantina?*

The city was already settling down for the night, the faceless walls of the buildings black on one side of the narrow street, a sheet of silver on the other. From some of the courtyards in the rear came the murmur of sleepy voices and, occasionally, muted wisps of laughter, but as

125

Luis moved away from the closely populated tenement section, the sounds of activity became ever more widely spaced.

The houses, too, were further apart, separated first by only the width of a wall, then by driveways and finally by vast moon-swept lawns and gardens. Luis was now in the finest residential district of San Luis where even the freshness of the air, the fragrance of the flowers smelled more expensive.

Just ahead was the Hacienda Morales, a massive square boxlike structure, flamingo pink where the entrance lights touched its stucco façade. Cars, like black beetles, lined the road in front of it. Luis could not yet hear the music, but he imagined that he could feel the drums throbbing in his brain with the rhythm of his own pulse. On the lawn in front of the hacienda, he could see the white shirts of the boys Señor Morales had hired to watch the cars. His muscles knotted with caution. Instinctively he began walking on tiptoe, staying on the opposite side of the street, stooped over so that the line of cars would screen him from the boys.

Because luck was with him he was certain the little señora's convertible would be here on the safer side of the street, and when he came upon its white, sleek metal body, he was satisfied that this was another good omen. Carefully, to make certain there was no mistake, he checked first the *turista* sticker, then the two little cloth dolls that hung from the inside mirror. It was the little señora's car all right.

He could hear the music clearly now, the stylized falsetto of the tenor, the clacking of sticks, the rattle of gourds and the slapping of the drums. Although his mind was unusually perceptive, his body seemed intent on betraying him. He found that he was breathing heavily and that, when he reached into his pocket for his knife, the palms of his hands were wet with sweat.

Quickly, before his cautious, cowardly muscles could destroy his will, he bent down and plunged the knife into the tire closest to him. The loud noise that the trapped air made as it escaped from the tire, the creaking of the car as it settled heavily on the unbalanced side, alarmed not only Luis, but the boys on the lawn. He could hear them talking uneasily as they moved toward the suspicious shadows on the moon-washed road.

"I don't see anything," one of the boys said in a high, tremulous voice. "Do you?"

A lone Roman candle, like the heraldic blare of a trumpet, whooshed into the sky and disgorged a series of red-and-white stars that lit up both the sky and the earth beneath it.

"It's as clear as day," the other boy said with relief. "You can see for yourself no one's there."

Luis crouched paralyzed with alarm until their footsteps retreated back to the sanctuary of the lawn, then his treacherous body urged him to run, to leave the job half-finished. He admitted to himself that it had been a close call, but he would not stop. He worked in a fever of anxiety, ripping the tough, loose rubber skin of the deflated tire until it was irreplaceable.

A protective firing of rockets had begun, covering up the sound of his movements so completely that when he punctured the second tire, he himself was scarcely able to hear its dying breath. The sky was magnificent with falling showers of red, green, white and yellow stars and even had they been able to hear anything, the boys on the lawn would have been too enthralled by the spectacle above them to notice it. Besides, like everything else that had happened in the last hour, nature itself conspired to help him. The setting moon moved down behind the trees taking with it the radiance that had touched the lawns and the road.

He moved to the front of the convertible, almost finished now. Having learned exactly what to expect, he waited for the whine of the rocket, the instant of explosion to plunge his knife into the left front casing. It was growing easier. His body, adjusted to the unfamiliar situation, proudly demonstrated its precision and skill. He was on the final tire when, from the noises around him—the exclaiming of the boys on the lawn, the musical trills that ended a number, the indistinct chatter of the guests—his hearing isolated an alien, unexpected one: the sound of running feet. No sooner had he identified it than a child's voice shouted, "Look, Papá!" and he knew that families were being drawn from the tenement district by the magnet of the fireworks. Even this, he realized immediately, was to his advantage. He could slip back through the protective darkness and lose his identity among the other spectators.

There was time only to puncture the last tire and retreat to the lawn opposite the Hacienda Morales before the dark forms began to spread out around him on the cool grass. No one noticed him and although he regretted being unable completely to mutilate the last tire, he was pleased with this final stroke of genius in becoming part of the anonymous crowd that gasped and sighed in unison at the brilliant aerial display.

From beginning to end he was proud of his own audacity and cunning. Now that the señora was unable to leave San Luis the emerald was as good as his. Who else could have found so clever a method of keeping her here? "God helps those who help themselves," he thought irreverently, half of his mind absorbed in pleased self-examination, reviewing his ingenuity, his flawless manipulation of circumstance, the other half following with childlike wonder the marvels in the sky.

The final barrage was exploding climactically overhead, disgorging cluster after cluster of shining stars. It ended with one cluster larger, more brilliant than all the

128

rest, that burst with a shower of glistening green stars that fell like a hundred emeralds sparkling in the night. This was another omen significant of wealth and good fortune. Luis wanted, suddenly, to share his delighted mood with others, congenial people like those in the *cantina*—Pepe who was so generous with drinks; the barmaid, Rosa, with the naked breasts under her thin blouse. Had she not invited him to stay? Had he not promised to return? He still had a few pesos. By tomorrow night he would be rich. Tonight he wanted to celebrate.

As soon as the fireworks ended, he started back to the *cantina*. He would buy Pepe a tequila, they would sing together, and maybe, later, he would go to bed with Rosa.

eighteen/

THE GUESTS watched the fireworks from the sheltered side of the terrace where a high, brick wall protected them against the sharpness of the wind. Beyond the terrace the gardens were a fairyland of bobbing Japanese lanterns, but the evening had grown too cold for anyone to occupy the small tables that had been placed there. The orchestra was still playing for the few couples who wanted to dance. At the buffet the pretty girls in their native costumes were still serving food. Juan, the good-looking boy who worked in the Villa Serena lounge, was still pouring wine. The sky was brilliant with artificial lights that for a few dazzling man-made moments outshone the stars. Yet the decelerated tempo of the music, the servants, the guests themselves indicated that the party was almost over.

"It must be after midnight," Jessie said. "Time to turn into a pumpkin."

Burt smiled at her. "Just one more round and then we'll go."

Because it was the last dance, each moment bubbled swiftly past with the effervescence of champagne. There were the sensual rhythm of the music, the romantic fragrance of the night, the grand finale of the fireworks crashing overhead and dying away like distant thunder, the last green cluster of stars like a shower of glittering jewels flickering toward earth, and with disappointing

130

abruptness the music stopped, the dance ended. The musicians started to pack away their instruments. The servants were clearing off the tables. All that was left of the magical evening were the lingering goodbyes, a final sip of Burgundy, and then with other guests from the Villa, they were outside at the car ready to leave.

"I feel a hundred feet tall," Burt said. "Either that or your convertible's shrunk."

From the back seat Emily's voice asked, "Burt, have you been drinking?"

"Not much," Burt said, starting the car and turning the wheel away from the curb. "Something's wrong." His voice was puzzled. "I think we've got a flat."

He climbed out again to look at the tires. "More than one, Jess. Do you have a flashlight?"

Jessie handed him the one from the glove compartment.

"By God," he said circling the car. "It looks as if someone's slashed your tires—all of them!" His astonishment and anger conveyed itself to the others in the car.

"But why would anyone want to do that?" Jessie was beside him, followed by Emily and Rose.

Other guests, realizing that something was wrong, joined them. Ruth Alexander was there asking, "What's happened, Jess?" And their host repeated over and over again with disbelief, "But I hired the boys to watch the cars." A man's truculent voice decided, "It must be the Communists," and the woman with him parroted the idea.

Everyone stood around not knowing what to do. Someone suggested calling the police, and their host, eager for any suggestion, hurried off to telephone. At the edge of the crowd of well-dressed guests, the shabby poor who had come to watch the fireworks, and had stayed to watch the departure of the guests, kept asking each other what was wrong.

Jessie, still under the spell of music and wine, stared without comprehension as the flashlight beam touched each of the shredded tires. The mutilation made no sense, had no reality for her. Words washed past her without meaning. As long as the shock lasted, she was protected against understanding what had happened, but when the delayed impact finally reached her, all the exhilaration of the party drained away, leaving her frightened and shaken.

She felt physically ill, chilled by the threatening darkness of the night, alone with the utter aloneness of the victim among spectators. Everything slipped out of focus. The mutiliation of her tires became an act of personal, insane violence, unexpected, like a blow from a friend, like the hostitlity that lay behind Dan's broad, automatic smile. The Mexicans who crowded in closer to see the damage ceased to be friendly, simple people who had come merely to watch the fireworks. The indignant voices around her belonged not to friends but to curious strangers whose words were meaninglessly garbled. For a long minute the nightmare of distortion lasted, then Burt's warm hand closed bracingly on her arm, reminding her of his presence.

The distortion faded. Familiar voices filtered through for recognition, yet the world did not completely lose its strange, four-dimensional quality. She continued to be aware of unknown lives and emotions that intertwined and conditioned her own. The ugly proof was there in the mutilated tires. Emily was saying that the violence was an act of political vandalism, a warning to all of them that they were not wanted here in Mexico, and although that impersonalized the menace, it simply underlined what Jessie was already thinking, that all of them were affected by forces beyond their control.

Still, when the policeman arrived, scattering the crowd with his motorcycle, she was glad to see him, hoping that he could find the culprit and that she would be able to see rather than imagine the face of danger.

The policeman's attitude was arrogant and self-contained, unsympathetic, as though it were Jessie's presence here in San Luis that was at the bottom of the trouble. Jessie heard the rasp of his questions, Burt's answers. She was asked to show her driver's license, the entry permit for the car, the Mexican insurance policy. Several times she heard the word "*comunista*" from the crowd, and each time it seemed to her that the policeman bridled and that his frigidity toward her increased. He drew the questioning out, inspecting and reinspecting her papers before he finally returned them to her. He turned at last to talk with the Mexicans, but they had melted away, all except the two boys who had been hired to watch the cars—and they, of course, had seen nothing.

"There's nothing more we can do, Jess," Burt said gently. "We'll have someone come for your car in the morning." Turning to Becky Groom he asked, "Can we all squeeze into your car?"

"Sure. There's lots of room."

On the way back to the Villa, Ruth Alexander reached over and took Jessie's hand. "I'm terribly sorry about all this, Jessie."

"It's not your fault, not anyone's fault," Jessie managed.

"I've never heard of such a thing before," Rose said indignantly.

"You have indeed," Emily snapped. "It's common enough everywhere these days."

They were all too excited to go to bed; uneasy, too, as if the action against one tourist was directed against all of them, and when they reached the Villa, they were reluctant to separate. Ruth suggested that they stop in the lounge for coffee. Burt lit a fire and they sat around it, saying little at first, but glad of each other's company.

"That policeman seemed to dislike me," Jessie commented at last. For some obscure reason the man's attitude disturbed her more than the ripped tires.

"He's probably a Communist himself," was Rose's comment.

"More likely we got him out of bed," Emily corrected.

Burt appeared to be less affected by the incident than any of the others. "Let's face it," he offered reasonably. "To the policeman it's not a serious crime. No one was hurt. After all, if it happened to anyone else you'd all agree that it was an isolated instance of violence. It is, you know. There's a crackpot minority anywhere—at home, abroad, here."

"Maybe. You read about something like this in the papers, but it never happens to you. It's different when it does," Jessie insisted. Her initial impressions of Mexico were racing through her mind, the feeling that she was in an alien, unfriendly land . . . the dry, hostile landscape . . . the flat, unfamiliar faces of the Indians. The Mexico of the tourist, she realized with fleeting perception, is a world within a world. Outside of the Villa Serena lay the real Mexico, the world in which threatening things happened like the murder of the Randalls and the slashing of her tires. "I've been in Mexico only three days," she continued. "This morning my purse was snatched, tonight— well, you all saw the tires."

"Jessie, I've been here for years and I've never had so much as a peso stolen," Ruth Alexander interjected. "Perhaps that balances it out."

"The chances are one in a million of its ever happening again," Emily said briskly, pouring everyone more coffee.

"One in five hundred thousand," Rose corrected her with an impish grin. "But I agree, Emily, it won't happen again."

Talking it over reduced the incident to the predictable status of a highway accident; still, a lingering uneasiness

134

held them together in front of the brightness of the fire. The conversation shifted to the party, its pleasures recreated and explored until the undercurrent was dissipated in the memory of the music, the food, the fireworks, the warmth of the hospitality. The mutilated tires were not mentioned again nor the threat implied in them. Only Jessie thought about them, wondering, from time to time, how difficult it would be to have them replaced and whether it would be very expensive, but she didn't mention them either.

While they were still talking the night dwindled away. The servants returned to the Villa. Uncle Pedro locked the gate and shuffled past the lounge on his way to the servants' quarters. The fire burned down to embers. Outside, the darkness grew less opaque until the slope and the wall became discernible through the grayness.

"It's almost sunrise," Ruth said at last. "You can already see the trees."

Her comment was all that was needed to remind the Grooms that they were very tired, and within a few minutes the group had scattered.

"For them," Jessie thought warily, "the whole business is over. For me it's just beginning." Some of the earlier nightmare significance returned, some of the odd, frightening dislocation, so that she was glad when Burt offered to walk with her to her door, past the threatening darkness of the bushes, the unknown and the unseen that hid in the shadows.

The wind had died and the pre-dawn stillness was broken only by the sleepy twittering of the birds.

In a few hours it would be daylight and something must be done about the car. Forced to face the problem, it seemed insurmountable. She was handicapped by her inability to speak the language and by a stubborn mental block that prevented her from even remembering her tire size.

"I don't know where to begin," she said aloud and some of her anxiety crept into her voice.

"Don't worry about your car, Jess. I'll take care of it in the morning," Burt reassured her.

"But could there be any trouble getting tires, I mean," Jessie persisted.

He started to answer her frankly. "Possibly. It depends on how many we'll need, whether we can salvage any of the old ones and what's available in San Luis." Then, noticing the chagrin creep across her face, he added firmly, "Look, Jess, I told you not to worry. At the very worst we'll have to order them from Mexico City."

"But that could take forever!" Jessie protested. For a single, vivid instant it seemed to her that without her car she was helplessly entrapped.

"Not forever, Jessie, an extra day or two at the most." He continued soothingly as if she were very young and very frightened. "Just remember, nothing serious has happened—nothing that couldn't happen anywhere and nothing that can't be repaired. Now, before it gets too hot, you get some sleep and leave the rest to me."

All at once, before she could respond or object, he leaned over and kissed her on the mouth. The warmth and closeness of the Cathedral were unexpectedly between them. His tenderness comforted her, made her feel safe and protected. It routed the dark wisps of her fears as effectively as the golden wash spreading near the horizon was routing the purple wisps of night. In the shelter of Burt's arms it was difficult to believe that anything could ever harm her. And, in the coolness of the early morning, it was equally difficult to really believe in the inevitable heat of the day.

nineteen/

BEFORE DAWN Inspector Menendes crawled out of bed. Although he moved quietly so as not to awaken Theresa, before he had finished dressing she was up, covering her plump body with the flowered housecoat.

"She's going to start again," the inspector thought gloomily, looking at her sullen, sleep-rumpled face and bracing himself against another tirade.

But Theresa left the bedroom without speaking. She moved heavily around the kitchen, banging the pots, clattering the dishes as if to emphasize the fact that she meant every word she had already said. A night's sleep had obviously not changed her opinion that her husband's bumbling had lost them a great deal of money.

The inspector realized that he had brought it all on himself. Never, never should he discuss his cases with Theresa. It gave her the privilege of asking questions and forced him to give answers. Last night, as soon as he opened the front door, before he had time even to remove his shoes or loosen his tie, she had asked whether it was true that Lieutenant Jiminez had made an arrest.

"I heard it on the broadcast," she said, as though expecting him to deny it.

"Yes, a suspect was picked up. It was a routine matter," he explained. "I was too busy to make the arrest."

137

"But the lieutenant wasn't too busy, nor will he be too busy to collect the reward," she said angrily.

"I suppose not," he had answered laconically. "If the man really is the murderer and if the jewel is found."

"And you don't care?" Theresa's voice squeaked with indignation. "It doesn't matter to you that María and I have to do without things when you could have so easily arrested the man yourself?"

"You don't really do without much," the inspector answered dryly, waving his hand at the ornate furniture that crowded the living room.

It was the wrong thing to say. Theresa enumerated the age of every piece: the chair had been given them by her mother; the couch was ten years old; the coffee table was a wedding present; the rug was threadbare; the stove was a prehistoric relic. The flood of complaints was followed by a flood of tears that stopped only when he assured her that, in the morning, he himself was going to search for the jewel, and that, if he found it, they too would share the reward.

Since it would be only part of the reward, Theresa had obviously decided to be only partly mollified. She poured him warmed-over coffee to point out the economies she was forced to practice and burned his eggs to remind him of the age of the stove; but, fortunately, she said nothing.

He ate with stolid concentration, listening for the arrival of Sergeant Roberto with the police car, and, at the first honk of the horn, he was outside in the crisp, early air. He imagined he could still hear Theresa banging the dishes behind him, but his mind had already leaped ahead to the village, anticipating the questions he would ask there.

In less than an hour they had turned off the main highway to follow the arroyo that the old Indian had described. During dry weather the arroyo made a smooth, efficient road, but its rippled sandy surface indicated that

138

rain would transform it into a swift torrent. It cut across a treeless countryside that had, in spite of its barrenness, a rocky, austere beauty. The huge, red disc of the sun pushing its way above the rim of the hills turned the slopes from purple to gold, touched the rocks with sequins, and brought with it an oven blast of heat.

The car skirted open range where skinny cattle stared after the passing car with gentle, incurious eyes. Stunted cornfields with thin, withered stalks as yellow as the earth itself began to stretch on either side of the gully. A black cloud of gnats beat against the windshield as they passed a garbage dump, and then they were at the village, a poor village of adobe huts set in the middle of the cornfields. A few trees showed the presence of a spring, but the lack of vegetation around the huts gave the impression that the land was completely arid.

Everyone rushed to meet the car, the half-naked children followed by rangy, silent dogs, the adults, even those at the far end of the fields, hurrying through the corn carrying their tools. Apparently the arrival of a car was an unusual event in the life of the village. The children stared at themselves in the shiny chrome bumper, nudging each other and giggling. The adults stared at the inspector. Who had ever before seen such a rich Indian in such fine city clothes? The sergeant's black uniform touched them with apprehension and they avoided him, but to the inspector they were very friendly.

It was easy to locate the old man's grandson, impossible to talk with him alone. The inspector had to adjust himself to ignore the circle of children and dogs that followed them everywhere they went, but the presence of the others did not disturb the boy, who looked at the inspector with round, intelligent eyes and answered his questions in a solemn, adult manner.

Much as the old man had told it, the child described how they had found the ring, leading the way across the arroyo to a knoll studded with dwarfed, twisted trees. Blending with the color of the ground so that it appeared at first glance to be nothing more than a pile of mammoth rocks was a weather-eroded idol, its features almost obliterated by time until only the general contour of the round head and kneeling body remained.

"It is here we found the ring," the boy said. "We left the grain and when we returned, the ring was there."

"And you saw no one bring the ring?"

"My grandfather says the god is still alive and left it for us. But my grandfather is very old."

"What do you think, boy?" the inspector asked gently.

The boy leaned over and picked up a handful of pebbles, throwing them one after another into the dry riverbed below.

"I don't know," he said uncertainly. "I asked the teacher. He said that maybe a bird stopped to eat the grain and dropped the ring there. Some birds, he says, carry things for many miles. . . . I know where there's an eagle nest, would you like me to take you there?"

"Not this time, son—later, perhaps."

Before they left, the inspector talked to many of the other villagers. He found that they were worried about the old man's absence, fearing that he had fallen somewhere in the hills and died. He was considered very feeble; some said that his mind wandered. It was rare for him ever to leave the village.

The circuit teacher came while they were still there, wearing the same loose, cool cloths as the other Indians, his books strapped to the back of his burro, a young, recent graduate from the University eager to change the world. He said the old man was dimwitted, steeped in ignorance and superstition, knew nothing of the progress of the outside world. He spoke rapidly in Spanish so that many of the elders around him couldn't understand his words. "Imagine," he said, "telling the child a god left that ring. Filling the young one's head with nonsense like that."

"There you have it," the inspector said, summing up the results for Sergeant Roberto as they headed back to the highway. "We have part of the ring and we have an Indian—the wrong part and the wrong Indian."

"How can you be sure that they're not all lying?"

"The circuit teacher . . . why would he lie? The child? He would say nothing. The other villagers? I asked them only about the old man and each of them had the same opinion, his mind is failing, he knows little of the outside world. Consider, Sergeant." He was speaking more to himself than to Roberto. "The planned nature of the crime . . . a murder, so nearly like an accident that it could almost pass for one. The theft of only money and a piece of jewelry. Does this add up to what we know of the old man?"

The sergeant shook his head. "No . . . I suppose not. Where does this leave us?"

"Back where we started . . . at the village near the highway. The Indians in that village do business with the tourists. They saw an identical accident at that curve. They know what happened afterward. This murder had to be planned by someone who knew what to expect. Look how carefully he protected himself. He even recognized the danger in keeping the ring. He figured the emerald could not be identified . . . but the mounting, that was something else again."

"So now we look for the emerald," the sergeant said cheerfully, simplifying everything.

The inspector glared at him, irritated by his optimism. "It sounds easy enough," he said sharply. "But where would you find it? It's flat, easy to hide, easy to disguise. Right this minute some Indian girl could be wearing it in a piece of native jewelry. It could be miles away. We'll try, all right, we'll plan our raid for tomorrow—but let's

141

face it," he ended bitterly. "We might never find the jewel."

He lapsed into moody silence not seeing the dun-colored hills speed past or noticing that the sergeant was driving far faster than the limits of prudence. He was thinking of the emerald, its size and thickness. Again he was trying to imagine a plausible hiding place that had not been searched, and, without understanding his own mental association, he thought, in an odd *non sequitur*, of the guide. He saw again the man's narrow, handsome face, the uneasy eyes, the greed that animated his expression when he heard of the emerald's value. He saw again the blue sapphires, the colorless crystal, the purple amethysts unpacked and spread across the desk.

"That guide," he said aloud. "He still worries me."

The words were lost in a screeching of brakes as they turned out of the arroyo onto the main highway. Two Indian women waiting at the road for the San Luis bus, with woven cages of live chickens beside them, were covered by a cloud of dust. There was no one else on the road or on the slopes beside it, yet Sergeant Roberto narrowly missed them. "That was close," he said. "Wherever do they come from?"

"Back in the hills where the conquistadors drove them," the inspector answered coldly. "You might slow down. These days the roads belong to everyone." He watched the speedometer for a while, his bulldog mind holding tenaciously to the severed links of his thoughts. "The guide," he insisted. "Could he possibly fit in anywhere?"

"I don't see how," Sergeant Roberto said. "Every minute of his day's been accounted for. I've checked it all myself. The tourists who were with him said he bought nothing at the village, but if he did buy the jewel from the Indians, where did he hide it? We searched the gas station, the café where he had lunch, his room—and found nothing."

"You searched the village, too, and found nothing," the inspector said acidly. "Yet we know that it must have been someone there who stole the ring and pried the emerald from the mounting."

"But you said yourself it could have been hidden anywhere away from the village—up in the hills."

"True, I was talking of the ring. Why would an Indian hide the stone if he were sure it could not be identified?"

The inspector stared out of the window at the monotony of the road, the kilometer markers whisking past, each indicating the diminishing distance to Mexico City. They were nearing San Luis, overtaking carts and burros loaded with produce. It was drawing it pretty thin to try to connect the guide with the crime just because he had been in the village. There was no evidence to justify it—only the avarice of his eyes when they discussed the value of the ring.

"What sort of a man is the guide? How does he live? What is he like? You must have found out something about him when you searched his room and talked with the tourists."

This sort of question always upset Sergeant Roberto. "Dog questions" he called them. The inspector expected him to sniff the air and come up with a reaction like a dog. He groped for the kind of answer the inspector wanted. "He likes clothes," he said. "Expensive ones. He has as many as a movie star. . . . And women, he talked to me about women. The *turistas* like him. I saw that for myself. He showed me a gold watch that one had given him, a beautiful woman from New York—blonde, he said—who stayed in San Luis almost a week."

The inspector grimaced, both at the image of a perfumed, ingratiating Luis and at the envy in the sergeant's

143

voice. They passed the gas station, the white-and-green pumps glistening in the sun. A huge, overloaded freight truck was just pulling in. "This where you arrested him?"

"Yes—right there. He was talking to a *turista* in a white car and I picked him up as soon as she left. She gave him a tip—fifty pesos—and he was with her only a minute. I saw it myself." Again his voice expressed amazement and admiration for the ease with which Luis could earn such a large sum of money.

"How did he act when you picked him up, anything in his behavior that was off-key—even a small thing?"

"No . . . he acted much as anyone would, objected but came along willingly enough." He hesitated, groping for an impression. "He was nervous."

Nervousness alone meant nothing. The inspector knew that it was rare to arrest a man armed with the calm of complete innocence, for who does not carry within himself the burden of buried guilt?

"Was he more nervous than they usually are?" he asked, recognizing, as soon as the words were spoken, the futility of asking.

The sergeant shrugged. "Who can tell? He was sweating in that heavy coat. He talked naturally enough. Anyway," he concluded logically, "he had nothing to be nervous about. He didn't have the jewel. He hadn't heard about the murder until you told him yourself. There was nothing on him except those cheap stones that are sold anywhere. I emptied every bag, unfolded every piece of tissue paper. You know there was no emerald there."

They were crawling through the outskirts of the city. Although it was only ten o'clock it was already intensely hot and the cobblestoned streets were jammed with pushcarts, children, errand boys on bicycles balancing huge trays of unwrapped bread or pastry, women with shopping baskets. An expectant, legless beggar on a wheeled plank raced along the sidewalk beside the huge black car until the inspector, absentmindedly, tossed him a few centavos.

It was the stones, the inspector realized, that made him think of the guide at all. The emerald would be about the same size, flatter, of course, with sharper planes, but small enough so that, once hidden, it would be almost impossible to find. "I'll never find it," he thought pessimistically. "Theresa won't get her stove. . . . And I won't get my murderer."

They circled the busy Plaza, passed the gray Cathedral with bells ringing for High Mass, turned left through the crowded alleyways and were, at last, at the police station. Here the street was almost deserted, no peddlers, no carts, none of the loiterers who cluttered the shaded steps of other public buildings.

"Tell me, Inspector," the sergeant asked as he opened the car door. "What ever made you think of Pérez?"

"I don't know," the inspector answered vaguely. "The loose stones, the unmounted jewel. The fact that he was at the village the morning after the Randalls were murdered and the ring was stolen. . . . Just grasping at straws, I guess. Come on, let's see if Lieutenant Jiminez has checked in yet. Perhaps he's had better luck than we had."

But the lieutenant hadn't even left. He was still at the police desk waiting for the inspector's return, obviously safeguarding his interest in the reward. "Well," he asked eagerly, "did you find it?"

"If you mean the emerald—no, we didn't," the inspector said flatly. "The old Indian never had the jewel, only the ring." And, before the lieutenant could ask anything else, he said sharply, "I thought you were supposed to cover the shops."

"I'm just about to leave. My schedule's on your desk —if you need me you can catch me anywhere on the route. My first stop will be Aguinaldo's."

145

AGUINALDO's was located not far from the cathedral on a small, completely naked, cobblestoned square grandiloquently called the "Plaza Milaflores." In the plate-glass window was a jumble of guitars, watches, brooches, crucifixes, statuary, beads of every size and color, clocks, cameos, all crowded together so that not an inch of display space was wasted. Inside the shop, except for the workbench set aside for the silversmith, the room was aisled by cases crammed with serapes and shawls, tablecloths, silver tea services, tray after velvet tray of rings, etched cigarette boxes of all shapes and sizes. An occasional stranger drifted in, as Rose and Emily had, to buy something or to have a piece of jewelry made, but mostly the shop was frequented by the people in the neighborhood.

Here Luis came for gifts on his mother's saint's day, here too, he had bought Carmelita's comb, and once he had sold Señor Aguinaldo a camera that a tourist had left behind in the rented car. It was a fine camera, made in Germany, with a special telescopic lens, and although Señor Aguinaldo had not paid what it was worth, he had given Luis a fine price for it and he had asked no questions.

It was only natural that this morning Luis would think

146

of Aguinaldo's. He had slept long beyond his usual hour and had been awakened at last by the ringing of the church bells, his mouth parched, his eyes sensitive to light, his head wincing with pain. "Never again," he told himself, recalling with distaste the rawness of tequila, the abandon of his voice singing with Pepe, the flower he had foolishly bought for Rosa. She had let him pin it onto her blouse and rub the softness of her breast. She had caressed him and called him "*Querido*," but at the end, when the *cantina* closed, she had left with that gross, overfed truck driver Gonzales. "The *puta!*" he said aloud and turned over on his side away from the light.

Pressing, importuning thoughts would not let him slide back into the comfort of sleep. He could hear his own voice bragging about his wealth, ordering drinks, until what he said and what he drank ran together in a river of drunkenness. With sudden foreboding he wondered whether he had spent the last of his pesos and jumped out of bed to search his clothes, finding in one pocket an empty, crumpled cigarette package, in another five centavos. For a second his poverty appalled him, then he found his knife, remembered the emerald, the reason for his celebration, and the ominous, sleep-ridden mists cleared. The jewel was as good as in his pocket right now and the squandered pesos were of little importance when Luis remembered that after today he would be rich.

Rich or not, he realized belatedly, today he would have to eat, tomorrow, too, and perhaps for many days after that until the jewel could be safely sold. He wondered about returning to the gas station and knew, as certainly as he had known yesterday, that he would not be permitted to wait there for the tourists. It was possible to pick up an occasional tour at the hotel, but after paying a *mordida* to the desk clerk, the remaining pesos would offer, at best, a marginal existence. No, in order to live he would have to sell one of his cherished possessions, his coat, perhaps, or his watch.

He took the handsome coat from his closet, stroked its fleecy softness, looked again with admiration at the Bond Street label sewed into the lining and decided that, after all, he could not bear to part with it. The coat could not be replaced. If anything were sold, it would have to be the watch.

It was an expensive watch, very slim, very elegant, with a narrow gold band that matched the case. The image of the elderly, lonely woman who had given it to him had become so blurred by Luis' description of her as a beautiful, blonde *turista* that now he almost believed he would be selling a romantic keepsake. However, he thought practically, the watch, unlike the coat, could be duplicated and, if something had to be sold, it would have to be the watch.

He had been told that the jewelers along the Calle Madero offered the highest prices for used jewelry, but there he might be expected to produce a bill of sale. He would have to shop, as usual, at Aguinaldo's; besides, soon he would want to sell the emerald and where else in San Luis could he dispose of an expensive item like that?

Today the shop was in complete disorder, the workbench torn apart, the counters piled high with things that had been pulled out of the cases, trays of beads overturned, rosaries tangled with earrings and bracelets in spiteful confusion. Sighing because of all the work before her and because her tiny feet hurt under the weight of her unrestrained body, Señora Aguinaldo was sorting through the piles with her fat, white, ring-covered fingers.

Señor Aguinaldo was fluttering around the workbench trying to help the silversmith put things in order, his face creased by a perpetual frown. He took Luis' watch, held it to his ear, examined the works with a jeweler's glass, then said, "Two thousand pesos, that's all I can give you."

Luis reached for his watch. "It's gold," he protested. "Solid gold. It's worth more."

"My friend, believe me, no one will pay more. Just yesterday I bought one like it for eighteen hundred pesos, only the band is not as nice as this one. . . . Where is that watch, Annamaría? Show it to the gentleman!"

His wife scrabbled through the debris on the counter, trying to find the watch.

"You must excuse us, Señor," Aguinaldo said. "The place is in an uproar this morning."

"It looks as if it's been torn apart."

"It was." Aguinaldo's frown deepened and he lowered his voice although there was no one else in the store except his wife and the silversmith who was silently getting back to work. "Lieutenant Jiminez was here just now —from the police. He's after a stone, an emerald." He lowered his voice even further so that it was scarcely more than a sibilant whisper. "It belonged to a murdered *turista* and the lieutenant says it's somewhere in San Luis. He threatened me. Imagine! He said he knew that I was a receiver of stolen goods!"

His volume increased with his indignation, but underneath there was a contagion of fear. It hovered in the silence when he paused, re-creating the presence of the police in the hot, airless shop so that the señora began to cry as she tried to untangle the jewelry on the counter. The silversmith stopped working to watch them with dark, calculating eyes like those of the Indians in the village or, Luis thought, like the eyes of the inspector across the scarred, yellow desk.

Strangely enough Luis was only lightly infected by the miasma of fear. Imperceptibly, as his determination to get the jewel had hardened, Luis had also hardened. Al-

149

though the word "police" would never lose its power to alarm him, it had lost the power to terrorize him. He was merely wary, weighing what was being said to see if, in any way, it could endanger him.

Aguinaldo was talking again, loudly, as if it were important to convince them all of his innocence. " 'I've always been an honest businessman,' I told him. But you know the police—they believe no one. This is the second time they've been here this week. 'If you know anything about the jewel and don't tell us,' the lieutenant said, 'I'll pull you in as an accessory to the murder.' An accessory, me! If I knew anything, why wouldn't I tell them? They don't have to do this," he ended morosely. "Well, what can you do? . . . Come, come, Annamaría, did you find the watch?"

Without thinking Luis had slipped his own watch back onto his wrist. As the shopkeeper continued to talk it became increasingly obvious that he was under suspicion and it occurred to Luis that merely being here could draw him into the orbit of that suspicion. He wanted to get away from the infectious surroundings, past the barrier of the counters, out into the hot, bright freedom of the streets.

But Aguinaldo would not let him go. "What is the matter, Señor?" he asked. "Just a minute. Don't run off. Maybe I can manage a little more. You've been a good customer. Twenty-two hundred pesos for the watch."

Luis hesitated. Twenty-two hundred pesos. He would need at least that much. Obviously, with the police searching everywhere in San Luis, the jewel could not be sold here. He would have to go to Guadalajara where he could stay with his family in the rooms behind the leather shop until he could find a buyer for the emerald. But, though he needed the money, was it really safe to leave anything behind that could link him with Aguinaldo?

"Twenty-three hundred pesos," Aguinaldo said firmly. "That's positively my last offer."

Luis' new courage asserted itself. Without speaking he slipped off the watch and handed it over, receiving in return a sheaf of pesos. You can't live dangerously, he assured himself, without taking risks, and, secretly pleased with his own temerity, he shook the shopkeeper's hand.

Now that he had money again, Luis realized that he was ravenously hungry. He stopped at the first restaurant, noticing neither the dirt on the floor nor the flies that buzzed around the sticky counter. Postponing all serious thought he ate until he was comfortably full and drank cup after cup of hot, bitter coffee.

Then he reviewed the scene in Aguinaldo's shop, contemptuous of the fear in the shopkeeper's voice, of the police who were fruitlessly searching for the stone, and smiled with secret amusement at the idea that he alone, out of all the people in San Luis, knew where the jewel really was.

He fumbled in his pocket for a cigarette, drew out the empty, crumpled package and for no apparent reason he pictured the little señora opening the tobacco pouch, emptying the contents and finding the emerald.

"How could I have been so stupid?" Luis was shaken out of his complacency. "Of course she'll find it. She may already have found it. She'll show it to someone, a jeweler perhaps. The police will be called."

He could hear her explaining. "I bought it from the guide. I had no idea of its value."

The words in the shop took on a new, sinister significance. The police had threatened Aguinaldo with being an "accessory after the murder." Luis, they might decide, was the actual murderer. If the little señora found the stone, she held his freedom, perhaps his very life, in her hands. There was a chance, an outside chance that she didn't know she had it. "But I just can't take that chance,"

151

Luis thought grimly, facing, for the first time, the full, dangerous reality of his situation.

Perhaps if he had not believed that his entire future was at stake, Luis might have fled even then to Guadalajara without the emerald; perhaps, under no circumstances, could he have left without it. Who can tell whether a chain of events, once started, does not produce an immutable momentum of its own? Luis had grown to think of the jewel as his, and he did believe his future was at stake.

Every step he took from that moment forward was motivated by a twin need to protect himself and to recover his property. If he thought of the little señora at all it was without compassion, coldly, as an obstacle to his plans, a threat to his existence. With desperate boldness he plunged along the path he had chosen, undeterred by human considerations. And, in this, he was only following the pattern of other men who become the creators of destiny.

twenty-one/

It is undeniable that, out of the vast mass of men, some stronger, more ruthless than the rest do control the destinies of others around them. The mayor of San Luis was such a man. He had been in office for many years and, with each succeeding term, his power and wealth increased until there was scarcely a decision that was made without his sanction.

It has been said that the results of Mexican elections are tallied with a speed that exceeds that of the most efficient voting machine. A machine can tabulate the results six minutes after the polls have closed; in Mexico the results are known six months before the polls have opened. This could, of course, be an exaggeration, but it was certainly true that there was no prospect of the mayor ever being replaced.

The most powerful men in San Luis, the city attorney, the city purchasing agent, the chief engineer and the commandant of police, each influential in his own sphere, all deferred to him. Once each week they met at his home to offer recommendations, but their suggestions were just a formality. It was the mayor who decided what land would be acquired by the city, to whom an important contract would be given, which cases would be pressed in court, which dropped.

Today he was in a grim mood. He paced the width of

his study glowering at all his lieutenants, but the brunt of his displeasure was focused on the commandant of police.

"Your men are a disgrace to my administration," the mayor began immediately. "The Communists are running wild. Last night, right here in my own neighborhood, a North American guest of my friend Ramón Morales had the tires of her car slashed."

The commandant, who had come directly from the bed of his mistress to the meeting wtihout stopping at headquarters, was taken completely unawares. "I knew nothing about it, *Alcalde*," he stammered.

"It's your business to know. Why should I, the mayor, know the details of this disgrace and the commandant of police be ignorant of it?"

"It concerned a tourist, you said." The commandant had found a hole to squirm through. "Tourist affairs are handled by Inspector Menendes. He's sent directly from the capital."

"I don't care who handles tourist affairs, or where he comes from," the mayor said, but his tone was a shade less belligerent. "We don't want to offend anyone from the capital, but this is a local affair, an obvious attempt to discredit me personally. I want the matter investigated."

"It will be investigated. Within twenty-four hours you will have a detailed report," the commandant promised.

The mayor said no more about it. The matter was forgotten as the meeting dragged on. The commandant was invited to a leisurely luncheon on the patio overlooking the mayor's magnificent rose gardens and swimming pool, and it was not until late afternoon that he remembered to call Inspector Menendes.

The inspector was working on a detailed plan for the search of the Indian village. Tomorrow would be, he was convinced, his last chance to find the murderer and he

154

wanted to be sure that nothing would be accidentally overlooked. A huge map showing the new highway and the network of roads in the area was spread out across the scarred, yellow desk. Small X's indicated where the police would start, simultaneously, at both ends of the village. Other X's showed the points at which the access roads leading off into the hills would be blocked. He and Sergeant Roberto were discussing how many men would be needed for a speedy, successful operation when the phone rang and the commandant's overly cordial voice intruded on their planning.

"Congratulations, inspector, on solving the Randall case. I know you're busy winding up details, but I'm sure you won't mind doing me a very small favor."

"We haven't solved the Randall murder, Commandant."

"You arrested someone." The commandant sounded confused, as though he had been given misinformation.

"The wrong man . . . we let him go."

"Oh. I don't suppose you could have held onto him—just to keep the books clear." Then, hastily, "No, I suppose not."

"What can I do for you, sir?" The inspector was frozenly courteous.

"It's a small matter, but of personal importance to the mayor."

So the commandant was in trouble with the mayor again. The inspector smiled and raised an eyebrow at Sergeant Roberto, who had no idea what he found so amusing.

"A very unpleasant incident occurred last night at the home of the mayor's friend Ramón Morales," the commandant was saying. "There was a small birthday celebration and, during the party, some Communists slashed the tires of one of the guests. Happening so close to the mayor's house, it seemed—"

155

"What has this to do with me?" the inspector asked. "It sounds like a local political affair."

"It would be except that the guest was a North American—a *turista*," the commandant said smoothly. "And that falls into your province. I know, as a matter of routine, you'll investigate, but I would appreciate having a copy of your report to show the mayor."

The inspector sighed, reached for a pencil and pad, sat down at the desk and said wearily, "All right, who was it? When did it happen?"

He jotted down the information. "Will you hurry along my copy of the police report? I'll have something to you by morning. Until then, Commandant." He hung up and handed Sergeant Roberto the notes. "Prewitt . . . Prewitt . . . One of those outlandish Anglo-Saxon names. Seems to me we've had something else on a Prewitt."

"I'll check the master files."

While the sergeant was gone, the inspector turned back to the map. Six men, he thought, would be enough, but they must be special men, none of these inept political appointees. He wanted qualified policemen who knew how to search and preferably ones who could at least understand Nahuatl. Not an easy job to find men like that.

Sergeant Roberto was back. "Here it is," he said, handing the inspector a mimeographed sheet. "A Mrs. Prewitt had her purse snatched on the Plaza yesterday. Could it be the same woman?"

"Could be." The inspector glanced absentmindedly at the report. "What about Ramírez?" he asked.

"Sergeant Ramírez? For what?"

"For tomorrow's raid. He speaks Aztec, doesn't he?"

"A little. But what about this Prewitt woman?"

"Don't bother me with it. Just write some kind of

report for the commandant, something he can show to the mayor."

The telephone rang again and the inspector, still preoccupied, answered it automatically. "Inspector Menendes here."

He was unprepared for the nervous, effeminate voice that came across the wire. "I was referred to you by the operator, Inspector. My name is Vallejo. I run a shop off the Plaza. We make and repair jewelry. I have a ring here that might interest you."

"I'm not looking for a ring," the inspector interrupted.

"I know. But just to be on the safe side I thought I'd better tell you about this one. It was brought in for repair and the stone doesn't fit the mounting."

"An emerald?"

"Yes."

"We'll be right over."

At the word "emerald" the sergeant, who had started to fold the map, stopped to listen, rigid with interest.

"Let's go!" the inspector said excitedly. "It looks as if Lieutenant Jiminez has caught us a fish." And, immediately deprecating his own excitement, added, "Let's hope it's not a minnow."

Within minutes they were at the Plaza, blasting their way through the crowded streets with the police siren. The peddlers, shoppers, dogs, children all scattered resentfully to the narrow sidewalks and stared with sullen eyes after the official car. Some, drawn into the vacuum of its passing, raced after it to cluster around the door of the shop, peering in to see who was being arrested.

Everyone was disappointed: the people outside the shop who expected some excitement; the silversmith who thought maybe he would get a small share of the reward; the inspector who had been hoping that this was the break he needed. The call was a false alarm. The stone was an emerald, all right, but smaller than the one that would fit the Randall ring, clumsily cut and obviously imperfect.

"Well, that's that," he said dejectedly when they went back out into the cauldron of the street. "I should have known that it was too easy to be true." Yet he had been hoping, more desperately than he liked to admit, that this jewel would be the right one, that there would be no need for tomorrow's raid, a raid that he had come to believe was foredoomed to failure. The thought of going home depressed him. Once Theresa learned of his failure, her welcoming smile would shift to disdain and she would load him with reproaches. Somehow, of course, he would manage to get her a stove, but it would not be the same as finding the jewel. Aloud he said, "It's almost five. Why don't we stop for a *cerveza?*"

"How about the Plaza Bar? I'm in uniform, you know —and no one ever goes there except the tourists," Sergeant Roberto suggested.

"Yes, I know. . . . It's dark, and only tourists go there. . . . And, just incidentally, I suppose, it's air conditioned."

The bar was already filled with a noisy group of foreigners, the radio blaring, the parrot screeching his usual "*Buenas noches,*" but it was dark and above all it was cool. They found a distant corner in which it was relatively quiet, ordered some beer, and, as they always did when they were together, talked about their work.

Finding the jewel had become, for both of them, a matter of personal vindication, the sergeant because he was afraid that he had overlooked it in the village, the inspector because he was afraid that the sergeant had not overlooked it and that the whole framework on which he had built his case would collapse.

Sergeant Roberto asked the very question he was asking himself. "What if we don't find the jewel tomorrow?"

The inspector stared at the yellow liquid in his glass. "The murder will have to be written off. Oh, the jewel may show up someday, but it won't help us. . . . That's the trouble. You see, even if the books are closed on the Randall case it won't be over. In another month, another year, maybe, there'll be another 'accident' at the same spot. That's why we just about have to find the jewel."

"And the chances?"

"Not as good as finding the ring," the inspector said frankly, "but we do know this. The murderer thinks it can't be traced and for that reason can't have hidden it too carefully. Last time you might have missed it because you were looking for a ring. If the emerald is still in the village, we have a good chance of finding it." He drained his beer. "How about another, Sergeant?"

Sergeant Roberto shook his head. "I still have to get everything set up for morning—you said you wanted to arrive before daylight. And there's that report on the Prewitt woman for the commandant. By the way, what will I say?"

"Oh, the usual flowery things. The police are doing everything possible to uncover the criminal, an arrest is expected shortly. Just something to satisfy the commandant."

"Shall I mention the purse snatching or deal only with the tires?" The sergeant, who had started to rise, sat down again, and without waiting for the inspector to answer, continued in a puzzled voice. "Inspector, maybe I've been working with you too long. But it seems odd to me that you're dismissing this so lightly. It is a tourist matter after all."

"Yes, but right now I'm trying to solve a murder case. Besides," he said, signaling to the waiter for two more beers, "I might as well be frank about it. I don't care much about being involved in the commandant's political back-scratching. You get started on something like this and there's no end to it."

The waiter brought their drinks. "I really shouldn't," the sergeant said, but he took a sip and continued sheepishly. "Inspector, I've been thinking. It's just an idea, but it seems strange to me that out of all the tourists in San Luis, this one woman would have her purse snatched and her tires ripped both in the same day."

He had the inspector's attention now.

"I've been reading the series of lectures you gave at the University," Roberto said. "And over and over you stressed the fact that nothing in police work can be dismissed as coincidence."

The inspector was flattered. It had never occurred to him that the sergeant could be interested enough in his theories to dig old copies of them out of the files or, having found them, would consider them worth studying. "Yes, I did say something like that, something to the effect that hidden threads often tie together apparently unrelated events—but in this case what could the threads be?"

"Well," the sergeant began uncertainly, "it sounds pretty farfetched. But what if this woman is a spy—or a smuggler? Let's say she's carrying something valuable, dope, maybe, or a large sum of money that someone knows about. Her purse is stolen but returned without being rifled. The woman is alarmed and will probably leave San Luis before another attempt can be made. . . ."

"And what better way to stop her," the inspector picked up the line of logic and carried it on, "than to damage her car in some way?"

The sergeant nodded. Already his reasoning was beginning to sound melodramatic and stupid. "I said it was farfetched," he ended doubtfully. "You said she was a friend of the mayor's."

"Everyone is a friend of the mayor's," the inspector commented dryly. "It would be amusing, wouldn't it, if the woman turned out to be some kind of a criminal? It wouldn't hurt to check with the border and find out exactly who she is." He drained his beer, threw some money on the table. "I think I'll go back to headquarters with you. I'd like to recheck that map, and there may be some difficulty getting the men we decide on."

Underneath he knew that he was grasping at an excuse not to go home, that tonight, of all nights, he did not want to face Theresa's complaints, that his worries and her avarice could spark an explosion that later he would regret. In his own world of authority, planning the hunt for the jewel, he could at least maintain an illusion of optimism.

twenty-two

THE SUN had dipped behind the trees, its last rays trimming the leaves with shining lights. Cool shadows crept across the earth and, as always, after the torpid, silent afternoon, the Villa came to life. The sprinklers were turned on in the garden. Tourists who had stayed over for another night returned from shopping or sightseeing in town. New tourists arrived.

In the kitchen the maids were getting ready for dinner. In the lounge Juan was polishing the cocktail glasses. At the gate Uncle Pedro was bowing to the newcomers, showing them where to park the cars and helping them with their luggage.

To Jessie, who had spent the day waiting to hear from Burt, all the activity seemed faintly unreal, as if the tourists and the servants were players moving against the artificiality of a stage set. Through the breathlessly hot siesta hours the Villa had been deserted. Jessie had wandered restively from her room through the garden to the lounge and back again without seeing another person and the emptiness had been a foretaste of what the succeeding days would be like without her car.

Although the exaggerated specters of the night before had retreated, she continued to feel vaguely entrapped. Rose and Emily were leaving for the States in the morning. Burt was overdue in Mexico City. The prospect of remaining here after them depressed her. With sudden

162

resolution she determined that, as soon as her car was available, she, too, would start for home.

"I won't think about what it will be like when I get there," she thought. "I'll just go back and face it."

The same desperate urgency that drove her to leave now impelled her to return. She went so far as to take her suitcase from the closet, realizing, only as she opened it on the bed, that since she didn't know when or how she could leave, it was ridiculous to pack. So she stood at her window watching the empty garden, and she was there when the first tourists arrived, still there when Burt returned from town.

As soon as he walked through the gate her spirits were magically lifted. She dashed out of her room, up through the thirsty garden to meet him, while he waited for her at the top of the slope. When she reached him, she could see, through the open gate, that he had driven her car back, that it was in the parking lot beyond.

"You did it, Burt! You're wonderful!" Her eyes were shimmering with delight.

"The car?" Burt grinned. "It was nothing that anyone with my brains, charm, and extraordinary ability couldn't have done. Seriously, Jess," he said, taking her arm and leading her out to where the convertible sat, "it's just a lashed-up affair." He pointed to the front tires. "I could only get two new ones. And the others—well, the left rear's your spare and it's not too sharp. The right rear is one that our friend only punctured. . . . For some reason it wasn't slashed like the others. . . . Lucky for you or your car would still be up on blocks." He opened the trunk. "This is an emergency spare—only that. It's the wrong size and bald, but if you have to, you can limp into a service station on it."

"Burt, I don't know how to thank you."

"Don't! You understand, Jess, this is only temporary. Replace that rear rubber as soon as you can."

163

"I understand. How far do you suppose it will take me?"

"Hard to say. Probably a couple of thousand miles. At least as far as Mexico City." He paused and looked at her intently. "You will go there with me, won't you, Jess?"

For a moment she thought he was joking, then she realized that he was seriously waiting for her answer.

"I don't know, Burt, I've been thinking about going home. It's what I should do. You told me that yourself."

"I did, but I'd like to have you go with me." He smiled wryly at his own contradictions.

Jessie evaded him gently. "When are you leaving?"

"I should have left today. I'll have to leave tomorrow. Think about going with me, Jessie," he urged.

She did think about it. Until the cocktail hour she thought about it. Her mind teetered back and forth between the alternatives until her resolve to return home began disintegrating. She became so irritated with her own vacillation that she almost despaired of the flaw in herself. It ended as it usually did without her being able to make any firm decision, and, when she finally left for the lounge, her suitcase remained open and untouched on the bed.

Darkness spread slowly across the sky until only a few pastel brush strokes were left to dramatize the western horizon. The usual evening breezes began to stir the bushes. One by one the guests gathered in the lounge where Juan, immaculate in his white coat and white smile, was pouring cocktails. It appeared to be an evening just like any other evening since the Villa opened.

But for Carmelita it was different. Her hasty temper had betrayed her again. A few angry words to the pastry cook and she was banished from the kitchen, assigned to make up the rooms for the night. Normally her banishment would not have bothered her, but tonight there was

164

a famous actress among the guests and Carmelita had been eagerly anticipating the dinner hour, when she would see her.

Now, with a pile of towels beside her, Carmelita waited on a bench in the outer darkness until the sounds of gaiety moved from the lounge to the dining room. Then, gathering up the towels, she started her chores. She told herself sullenly that she didn't really mind. One day soon she would marry Luis. As Uncle Pedro said, he was a good catch. He would take her away from the Villa, and afterward she would come back, dressed in fine clothes, and all the others would envy her.

However, ultimate triumph was no substitute for the present. Her movements were resentful as she moved from room to room, tidying the bathrooms, turning down the beds, lighting fires in each of the circular, tile fireplaces. The rankling thought of the other maids in the dining room, particularly the lucky one who would wait on the famous woman, destroyed even the desire to poke through the tourists' possessions.

In the actress' room curiosity overcame her resentment. Here was an experience none of the other maids could share, and, later, when they talked about the actress, she, too, would have something to say. She rubbed her cheek against the fluffy furs hanging in the closet, examined shoes with shining heels of glass, unfolded and refolded the gossamer lingerie in the dresser, opened the box of cosmetics and, beginning to enjoy herself, carmined her lips with one of the gold-encased lipsticks.

The evening was turning out better than she had expected and her good humor was completely restored when she found Juan waiting for her outside the door. Pretending not to notice him she started toward the next room. At his touch she squealed as though in fright, but her heart was skipping with happy excitement and she was unable to conceal her pleasure. With only token resistance she responded to his importuning lips and forgot, instantly, her intention of marrying Luis.

From number twenty-four Luis could hear her plainly, the tiny screech of fright followed by her laughter and finally her voice, purring with excitement, "No, Juan, not now. I have to do the rooms." There was the rumble of Juan's reply, sounds of a scuffle and Carmelita's voice again full of seductive promise. "Later, Juan. I'll meet you later."

Luis' mouth tightened into a narrow line. "The bitch," he thought. "The dirty bitch!"

He had been in the little señora's room for several minutes, padding restlessly around looking for the jewel. There had been no difficulty getting into the Villa grounds. He had chatted with Uncle Pedro until they were both certain that all the guests were in the dining room, then had stolen through the garden, crossed the lighted walkway and was once again in the large, airy room that smelled faintly of violets. Here he intended to wait until the little señora returned and when she did, he would get his jewel.

Although it was contrary to his every instinct to expose himself so openly to danger, he felt that he no longer had any alternative. Direct action was all that was left to him. He could not afford the luxury of devious methods, which might be safer but could just as easily prove fatal. Below the surface of his open thoughts Luis knew that once he had the jewel he could not let the little señora live, yet on the surface he kept telling himself that he did not intend to harm her.

There was a chance, a slim one, that he really would be able to avoid violence—if only the emerald were hidden in the room. Quickly but thoroughly he searched the open suitcase on the bed, the closet, the drawers, the bathroom—but it wasn't there. Once he was convinced that any further search was futile, he was strangely calm with a determination that was unlike him, as if, having reached the point of no return, excess emotion was superfluous.

He stood near the open window looking out into the darkness, watching the lighted strip of the walkway. He noticed the faint, peppery scent of the air, the intermittent croaking of the bullfrog who lived in the pool outside the window—and it was from here that he had heard Carmelita.

Listening to her slam the doors as she moved from room to room, Luis wondered how often after he himself had left the Villa and Juan had closed the lounge those two had met to lie together under the trees, maybe under the very tree where she had recently whispered lovingly to Luis.

Now she was in the next room. He could hear her banging around in there as if she didn't like the occupants. Something crashed to the floor, a vase, perhaps. He imagined her picking it up with supple movements, her dark hair falling across her face, a quiet, secretive smile on her pretty face.

He had an insane impulse to remain where he was, to surprise her when she entered the room, but prudently he crossed over to the closet, stepped inside, leaving the door slightly ajar so that he could watch her. She came in, humming to herself, and snapped on the overhead light. Her face was flushed, her eyes glowing. She was smiling just as he had imagined she would be and in her thick, black hair she was wearing the sparkling comb he had bought for her.

He could see her only while she bent over the small fireplace to light the fire, then she moved away from his narrow range of vision. He could hear the sliding sound of the curtains as she pulled them against the night. She was at the bureau now, running her fingers through the loose objects in the jewel box. She must have tried something on because she said to herself admiringly, "My, you are pretty, Carmelita." There was the faint clank of the object being returned to the box, a faint snap as she closed the lid.

She was directly in front of him again, coming toward the closet door. Unexpectedly the sweat broke out in the palms of his hands and he was breathing heavily, yet his mind remained calm and precise. If Carmelita saw him, even for an instant, she would recognize him. Without hesitation, slowly, noiselessly he slid the knife from his pocket, flipped open the blade and waited for her. When she opened the door he would plunge it into the hollow spot at the base of her throat, the spot he had so often kissed. He knew, suddenly, that he wanted to kill her, that he hated her for her betrayal of him with Juan, without remembering that he, also, had betrayed her, forgetting, even, that he had cared nothing for her.

She was at the door and he braced himself to move instantly, grinning at the thought of her astonishment when she would see him there, an astonishment that would last only the instant that she remained alive. Instead of opening the door, however, Carmelita shut it and Luis stood in muffled darkness, experiencing an immediate reaction of relief mixed with shocked amazement at his own traumatic urge for violence. Dimly, as though from a great distance, he heard the water running in the bathroom, Carmelita's footsteps passing the closet, felt rather than heard the front door close, and knew that she was gone. Still he stood in the closet, leaning weakly against the wall, shaken by the unacknowledged demons that stirred within him.

At last he re-entered the room, turned out the table lamp Carmelita had lighted and settled down to wait for the little señora. The writhing flames of the fire distorted the shadows so that they seemed to move eerily with a life of their own. With the fireplace behind him he didn't dare stand silhouetted against the window. Instead he sat in the easy chair, relying on his ears to warn him against surprise, and he smoked the señora's cigarettes, enjoying the mild Virginia tobacco, reconciled to the waiting.

Because he did not want to think of what would happen when the little señora returned to her room, he thought beyond it, to afterward when he would have the jewel and it would bring great changes. Until it was sold he would wait with his family in Guadalajara, then he would go to Acapulco. He had never been there, but he could imagine how the beach must look, like the California beaches, with silver-white sand and a green-blue ocean. He pictured himself sitting among the rich and favored on the terrace of a fine hotel, drinking something from a tall, frosted glass. He would tell everyone that he was looking for a place to invest some money. He would seek advice from the wealthiest and among them it should be easy to find an appropriate wife. It would be nice, of course, if she were pretty, but there were advantages in marrying a rich, homely woman, one who would be generous and grateful.

From time to time the present intruded on his dreaming, the sharp crackle of the fire or the noisy, unexpected sound of a bird shrilling in the garden. Then, reminded of the dangerous hours ahead, Luis would steel himself to think of what he would do when the little señora returned to her room.

When he heard her coming he would flatten himself against the wall near the door. As she entered he would grab her, cover her mouth before she could scream and force her to hand him the jewel. After that he would have to improvise, because each time he arrived at that point, his mind balked and would not go beyond it.

Instead it strayed into the future, or back to the past, to the fortuneteller and her prophecy about a great fortune and a woman from the north. Could it be possible that this emerald and the little señora were the fulfillment of the prophecy? What was it she said? "For each man there are many paths, and great riches and a woman can lead him down any one of them."

Thinking about it touched him with uneasiness so he forced himself to concentrate on Acapulco, imagining the sunshine sparkling on the ocean, the girls in their abbreviated bathing suits, and once again he almost forgot that he was in the little señora's room, smoking her tobacco and staring into the changing and changeless flames.

Dinner must be ending for a few people were already moving out in the garden and along the walks. Luis was alert, now, standing near the door tense with waiting, but the little señora did not come. Standing there, he was aware of the full enormity of what he was about to do and painfully conscious of the passing minutes. Fear, like the insistent droning of an insect, began to buzz in his mind, and he was unable to drive it away. If he could have fled, he would have, but there was no choice. He could face the señora now, or the police later. And face the police Luis could not do. So he waited while the toxin of fear spread through him, controlled only by his desperation, by his need to survive.

A couple came along the walkway and paused outside the door. For a moment he thought that it was the little señora and the man with her. "Could I have miscalculated?" he asked himself with panic. "Could it be possible that she would return to her room, not alone but with the tall, gray North American?" There was no time to return to his hiding place. He could only stand in an agony of fear and listen to the man's voice say, "Wait here, I'll get your stole." And the woman answer, "No, I'll come with you, I need to freshen up a bit." Then they moved on down the walk, the woman's slender heels clicking sharply on the flagstones like a metronome keeping time to the wild pulsing of Luis' heart.

twenty-three

SOME of the guests had already finished dinner, and the dining room was beginning to empty. Near the window the famous actress, lonely and aloof, lingered over her coffee. A middle-aged couple sitting nearby stared frankly at her and made comments on her appearance as though she were a mannequin who could neither hear nor see them.

At Jessie's table the cheerful fund of conversation was running thin, almost as if Rose and Emily were already on their way back to the States and Burt had left for Mexico City. "I'm the only one who's undecided," Jessie thought, vacillating again between following the teachers north and Burt south. Going home did not seem as easy as it had this afternoon when the date of departure was still remote. But, if she went to the capital, was it really because she wanted to be with Burt or was it just a further flight from Dan?

"Have you packed yet, Jessie?" Burt asked, and she knew that he was once again urging her to go with him.

Before she could answer there was one of those momentary hushes that occur unexpectedly in noisy rooms. This one was caused by the departure of the actress, who swept through the room leaving in her wake the scent of magnolias and a murmur of voices that probed, as they always did, the publicized tragedy of her marriages, the loss of her children, her reputed immorality.

171

"A woman like that," Burt said kindly, "is the victim of her own beauty."

"In my next incarnation," Rose declared, "I'd like to be victimized that way. They can say what they want about the rewards of virtue. . . ."

The waitress interrupted her. "Scuse, Señora." She was speaking rapidly in Spanish, but her eyes, wide in her thin face, were fixed on Jessie.

Burt appeared to be so puzzled that even before he started to translate, Jessie experienced the first knots of worry. "She says there are two men to see you, Jess. Would you like me to find out what they want?"

Jessie had already risen. "Something has happened to Dan," was her instant thought. She was aware, suddenly, of the blackness beyond the windows, as if the dining room were suspended on a sheer cliff. Aloud she said, "No, thank you. I'll go. Where are they?"

"In the lounge."

Trying not to anticipate trouble, forcing herself to remain calm and walk slowly, Jessie left the dining room, climbed the few steps to the lounge, and, as soon as she saw the men, the foreboding that had started at the table crystallized into certainty.

The large man was very dark, all brown it seemed, his suit, his shoes, his hat, his skin. In spite of his civilian clothes he was unmistakably a policeman. The man with him was in uniform, a young man, rather handsome with swarthy skin and startlingly pale eyes. They were standing uncomfortably near the door and the tourists in the lounge watched her approach in much the same way as they had watched the actress.

"Señora Prewitt?" It was the large man who spoke, his English very stilted and correct, with only a faint accent. "I am Inspector Menendes. This is my associate, Sergeant Roberto."

The young man clicked his heels and bowed smartly.

172

The inspector was opening the door. "If it is permitted, Señora, it would be more convenient to talk outside."

Without will of her own Jessie preceded them to the rustic chairs that were grouped on the terrace and sat down. The light streaming out through the windows of the lounge fell across them in huge squares that highlighted their faces and shoulders and left the rest of them in the shadows. Beyond them the garden seemed plunged into darkness except for the chain of lanterns that picked out the steps of the walk. The polished disc of the moon was barely visible behind the foliage of the ancient trees.

"We are here," the inspector began, "at the request of the commandant of police."

And Jessie, braced for bad news, had no way of knowing that the words were only partly true.

Actually a combination of circumstances had led the inspector to stop at the Villa. The arrangements for the morning's raid were completed earlier than he had anticipated and Theresa, he knew, would still be waiting up for him. Also, at Sergeant Roberto's insistence he had reread the police reports and, perhaps because the idea had been successfully planted, he wondered if there were not, after all, some connection between the events on the Plaza and the incident at the Morales home. It intrigued him to think how embarrassing an investigation would be to both the commandant and the mayor if the woman turned out to be a criminal. Sitting here, looking at her, it was hard to believe that this little woman with the anxious eyes and dignified manner could be involved in anything unsavory. But as the inspector knew, criminals come in all shapes and sizes.

"Tell me, Señora, about your car. Were you able to replace the tires?"

Jessie smiled with relief. "Oh," she said. "It's about the car."

"Why yes, Señora," the large man answered blandly. "What did you think it was about?"

"For a moment . . . I thought . . . perhaps something had happened to Dan . . . my husband," she explained.

"I'm sorry if we alarmed you. No, it's not about your husband. We are concerned about what happened last night. It must have been a frightening experience following so quickly after the theft of your purse."

"It was," Jessie agreed. "I'll admit that I was pretty shaken up. It was a small boy who stole my purse. I saw him myself. . . . But this other thing . . . not knowing who did it. It's true, it scared me."

Fragments of the experience returned to trouble her, the odd feeling that she was being threatened for reasons she didn't understand. Her perplexity showed plainly in her face.

"And now, Señora, you are no longer frightened?"

"No, I realize it could happen to anyone, anywhere. I just was unlucky, I guess. My car was in the wrong place at the wrong time."

"There isn't any reason then why anyone would want to harm you?" The inspector was leaning forward, carefully studying her face.

"No reason at all." The question was obviously unexpected.

The door to the lounge opened and one of the maids came out onto the terrace bringing them a tray of coffee and pastry. While she served them there was a static silence in which all the frightening implications of the inspector's questions seemed to gather form and substance in the night. They peered at Jessie from the blackness of the garden while the wind plucked at her with chill fingers.

"Very kind of the Señora Alexander." The inspector's polite comment reduced everything to the commonplace. "These cakes are delicious. The sergeant and I haven't eaten yet."

The sergeant nodded as though he understood what was being said but was unable to answer.

Not until the maid had left the terrace did the inspector say anything of importance, and, when he did return to the subject, it seemed at first as if his mind had veered off in another direction.

"You know, Señora, coincidence is a word that a good policeman does not easily accept. Has it occurred to you that the damage to your car was not merely the result of accidental selection?"

"But that's ridiculous!"

"Is it?" He took out a package of cigarettes, gave Jessie one and elaborately lighted it for her. "Tell me, Señora, are you carrying a great deal of money?"

Jessie smiled wryly. "Scarcely four hundred dollars—barely enough to stay in Mexico a few days and get back home."

The sergeant interpolated something in Spanish. The inspector nodded and said, "Sergeant Roberto says, and it's true, four hundred dollars is a huge sum of money to most of our people."

"Oh, but you don't understand. No one else can use it. It's in traveler's checks."

The inspector nodded solemnly as if he agreed that that was the only way to carry money. "And you have nothing else valuable? Jewelry, for instance?"

"Only my rings—they're not really valuable." She glanced down at the tiny solitaire that Dan had given her when they were still in school. She remembered with a momentary pang how wonderful he had seemed that day, how close they were, what wonderful dreams they built for the future.

There was a subtle change in the inspector's voice. "No one would snatch your purse for your rings, Señora."

"Inspector, I don't know what you're getting at." She was more angry than confused now. She had detected a veiled insinuation and, although she didn't understand its meaning, reacted against it. "Are you accusing me of something?"

She could not see the inspector's hands, but she had the impression that he had turned them palm up, much as a magician does to prove that he is concealing nothing. The expression on his face did not change, only his eyes seemed a little more penetrating.

"Señora, I'm simply searching for possible threads between these coincidences. There may be none. There may be some that you know nothing about. But I would be derelict in my duty if I did not try to discover them."

Jessie puffed at her cigarette in stubborn silence. She was surprised at the gentleness with which he continued.

"Señora, have you ever thought that nothing is unrelated, that everything has a beginning and a meaning, that things happen that we don't understand only because we don't know the reason for their happening?"

"I've thought of it," Jessie said quietly.

"I'm trying to find out why these things have happened to you—and when I do, perhaps I can find the people who harmed you. It's just possible that you have been mistaken for someone else," he suggested.

For a minute Jessie had been drawn into the magnetism of his logic, then, because she realized it was frightening her, she protested.

"Really, Inspector, I think you're reading too much into this."

"That could be," he said, remembering the genuineness of both her confusion and anger, and realizing that now he had upset her. "I don't mean to alarm you. There is probably nothing to be alarmed about. I am just trying to explore every possibility. Just one more question,

176

Señora. Are you, or have you ever been, involved in politics?"

So that's where the wind really lies, Jessie thought, and smiled broadly. "No, Inspector. I'm not a political person or even an important one. There was no glory to be gained in slashing my tires."

She stood up. "Gentlemen, if you have no more questions, will you excuse me. It's growing cold out here and I need a sweater."

The two men stood too. Inspector Menendes could tell that, in spite of her flippant reply, she was still disturbed and he blamed himself for it. Before leaving he wanted to soothe her. "Señora," he said, and one of those rare, charming smiles brightened his massive face, "I hope we haven't upset you. It is my duty, you see, to protect the tourists in San Luis. I would never forgive myself if, simply to save myself and you from embarrassment, I failed to ask questions that could expose anyone who threatened you. You have been most patient and kind."

He took her hand and raised it to his lips in the European manner. Sergeant Roberto, who had been able to follow the conversation but had missed the nuances of it, was so astonished by the inspector's gallantry that he almost forgot his military bow.

Jessie stood on the terrace watching them climb the steps to the gate. She had the peculiar feeling that the inspector knew things about her that she didn't know about herself and she was sorry that she had dismissed him so abruptly. From the distance she observed the discouraged slump of his shoulders. His cool detachment was forgotten; only the warmth of their final moments together remained. As though a deep understanding existed between them she felt a surge of empathy. She tried to recall his exact words, realizing, now that he was gone, that he had articulated thoughts that had sped elusively through her own mind during the last few days.

She was so preoccupied that she did not notice Ruth Alexander until she was standing beside her.

"I'm sorry I missed Inspector Menendes. He was here about the tires, of course," Ruth guessed shrewdly. "A very unusual man. Nothing that happens to a tourist ever escapes him."

"He seemed to think I was a criminal, or something," Jessie said.

"Nonsense—that's just your imagination."

"I don't know. He asked an awful lot of questions."

"Detectives make their living by asking questions, my dear," Ruth said. "This sort of thing is routine with the inspector."

"He comes here often?"

"He's been here before. Come on now, Jess. Rose is trying to organize a bridge game. Emily refuses to play. You'll take a hand, won't you?"

"Yes, after a while. I have to wash up first and get my sweater. And I should do just a little bit of packing."

But, as she walked down the lighted walkway to her room, she still didn't know why she should pack, because she really didn't know where she was going.

twenty-four/

THE FOOTSTEPS were as quick and light as those of a child, but long before they reached the room Luis knew that they belonged to the little señora. He pressed motionless against the wall and waited, holding his breath with an odd mixture of fear and anticipation. He had gone over it so often in his mind that he knew exactly how it would be, what she would look like when the door opened; yet when she walked through the doorway it was different, somehow. She was smaller than he had imagined. Instead of seeing her face, he found himself looking down at the shining cap of her head. The dim light from outside turned her hair to pale satin, fell in soft patches on her beige sweater, caught on the brass clasp of the purse and the matching brass ornament at her neck. Like her room, she smelled faintly of violets, and like her room, too, she was extremely neat. She came in quickly without noticing him, reached out to grope for the light switch, touched the fleecy surface of his coat and her fingers hovered there as if startled at the first warning of danger.

It all seemed to happen in slow motion, but before she had time to identify what she was touching, before she could even raise her head to look at him, he had seized her, one hand over her mouth, the other grabbing her firmly around the waist. With his foot he pushed the door closed behind them and they were alone in the room, both breathing heavily, their shadows grotesque and black on the firelit wall.

After the first immobilizing surge of paralyzing fright, Jessie fought wildly to free herself from the nightmare that had sprung at her out of the darkness. She thought only of the need to escape, scratching at the hands that held her, trying to tear them away. Then, because that was impossible, she tried to twist around to face her attacker, and it was when she failed to succeed that the full impact of terror overwhelmed her. The man behind her became monstrous and inhuman, the personification of evil, huge and dark with malignant eyes, hands that were possessed of superhuman strength. In the desperation of her terror she almost broke loose, kicking at him viciously, raising her hands to grope for his hair, his eyes, anything she could seize, but he continued to hold her until her store of strength ebbed away and she lay frightened and trembling in the support of his arms.

She could feel the rapid rise and fall of his chest behind her and knew that he, too, was exhausted by the struggle. Dimly, from the next room, came the sound of a radio, and voices filtered past the draperies that were drawn across the open window. Out in the garden there were people who would help her if only, she thought frantically, she could break free long enough to call for help.

He seemed to read her thoughts, for he said, "Don't scream, Señora, and I won't hurt you."

His voice surprised her. It was not as she had expected it would be, but soft, reassuring, and it filled her with hope.

"Promise me you won't scream, Señora," he insisted, tentatively loosening the hand that was over her mouth, waiting for her whispered promise, then releasing her completely.

She shrank back against the support of the wall to stare blindly at him without comprehension or recognition.

"She doesn't know me," Luis thought with amazement, forgetting that, although he had been watching her stealthily during the past few days, she had seen him only once, briefly, at the gas station.

"Your handbag, Señora," he said, smiling reassuringly at her.

The fear that clouded her vision slowly receded. She saw a tall young man in a full, tan coat with a narrow, handsome face that was vaguely familiar. She felt as though she should know him, but her mind and body were still stunned, unable to react normally.

"Your handbag, Señora!" His tone sharpened and she noticed for the first time that he was holding a knife, gesturing with it so that the firelight glinted on the blade, and the trembling inside her began again.

Numbly, with great effort, willing every movement, she held the purse out toward him, but he shook his head impatiently. She started to whimper because her fear was washing over her and she couldn't understand what he wanted.

"Open it!"

Her fingers tried to obey, fumbling with the catch awkwardly as though they were swollen. "I have nothing here," she said at last in a small, hoarse whisper.

For an instant Luis believed her. "She's found it," he thought. "I'm too late." Then seeing the wide blankess of her expression he realized that her fear had blocked out understanding.

"The stones," he prompted urgently. "In the tobacco pouch . . . in your handbag. Make it fast."

She was groping in the bottom of the purse, past the papers, the wallet, searching for the cloth surface of the pouch, feeling the sweat break out all over her body as she hunted for it. Her staring eyes never left his except to race swiftly to the menacing blade of the knife and back again. His face, the coat, the hand holding the knife, her own sweating anxiety all coalesced into a single image. She remembered suddenly who he was, how he had leaned over her car to throw the bag of stones into her handbag, how he had smiled at her and waved when she pulled away from the gas station, and involuntarily, she gasped, "You're the guide!"

Before it was fully formed, as if he were tuned into the same wavelength, Luis saw recognition blink through her terror. He watched her with fascinated detachment, knowing that, if she recognized him, he was going to have to kill her and that the thought was neither a new nor an unpleasant one.

She stopped hunting for the stones, frozen by what she read in his eyes. He was coming toward her slowly and she automatically backed away, sidling along the wall until she was trapped by the dresser. She opened her mouth to scream, but, as in a dream, no sound came out. She kept telling herself that she would awaken and the terror would be gone. For an instant she closed her eyes and willed herself awake, but, when she opened them, Luis was still there and she knew that she would not awaken. She was unable to make a move to protect herself. The pocketbook fell from her nerveless fingers scattering its contents on the floor, but neither of them noticed it.

Luis was drawn irresistibly toward her in a macabre dance of death, fascinated by her fear, exhilarated by a strange sense of power. They were so much a part of each other that they might have been lovers walled off from the rest of the world by their mutual absorption.

Beyond the partition that separated them from the next room someone was restlessly twisting the dial of a radio. Outside there were people strolling in the garden and along the stone walk, but the sounds were remote, without reality. Everything that lay beyond this room had ceased to exist for Jessie because she was, with silent terror, facing death, and for Luis because he was completely mesmerized by his power over her. When the knock on the door came, they were both equally startled.

"Answer them," Luis whispered. "Tell them to go away."

But Jessie, beyond the power of speech, beyond the ability to make a move that might save her, could only look at him, wonder why he was prolonging the eternity of waiting.

When she did not answer, Luis knew that the sands of his freedom were running out. He had an insane urge, impelled by the momentum of all that had happened between them, to fulfill his destiny with the little señora; but before he could move, the door behind him opened; someone rushed up behind him and pinioned his arms.

Without turning around, Luis knew that it was Inspector Menendes who held him. How he knew, he was never able to explain, but it seemed inevitable that if he were taken by the police, it would be the big Indian who took him. In retrospect it was as if the broad, stone-like face, the obsidian-hard eyes had been in the shadows of his mind as long as he could remember. Perhaps it had been in his father's mind, and his father's father's mind before him, an image that had a racial history that neither time nor the infusion of new blood could erase, but it completely terrorized him.

As soon as the inspector touched him, Luis was filled with such overwhelming, convulsive panic that he tore his way free, pulling out of his coat and running through the room, out the door and across the lighted walkway past Sergeant Roberto, who was leaning against one of the posts smoking a cigarette.

Behind him he could hear the bark of the inspector's

orders, the sergeant's shouts, but he continued to race up the stone steps through the garden, screened by the dark, protective bulk of the shrubbery. Pulling his leaden legs after him, breathing the sharp night air in painful gasps, he pushed himself toward the sanctuary of the gate.

The tourists walking along the lighted paths of the garden hurried toward the shouting to find out what was going on. Others were drawn from the lounge onto the terrace. The maids crowded out of the kitchen door. And, although they all looked in the general direction of the slope, no one knew what they were looking for. Only Uncle Pedro knew that a stranger must have gotten onto the grounds.

He heard the sound of someone running up the stone path even before he saw the moving figure approach him. In the darkness he could see only the blurred whiteness of the shirt and picking up his heavy club he rushed wildly at the approaching man. It was only after he had struck him down that he recognized Luis; then he was completely confused by what had happened.

He was holding the guide's bleeding head on his lap when Sergeant Roberto arrived. "I didn't mean to hurt him," he said apologetically. "I didn't know him without his coat."

"How did he get on the grounds?" the sergeant asked, and from the tone of his voice Uncle Pedro realized that Luis must be in serious trouble.

"I let him in," the gatekeeper said.

"You let him in? Do you just let anyone in?"

"Oh, no," Uncle Pedro said, sorting through his mind for a reasonable excuse, and using the one that Luis himself had so convincingly given him. "But you see he came to see the Señora Alexander. She owed him a *mordida*."

"He'll get more of a *mordida* than he bargained for," the sergeant said, helping the guide to his feet. "Keep an eye on him. I'm going back to get the inspector."

Long afterward, when Inspector Menendes had unraveled all the threads and rewoven them into a cohesive tapestry, he marveled at the narrow accident of timing that had led him to the jewel. His immediate concern, however, was with the woman whom he found still enmeshed in the cobweb of horror. Blind with shock, she continued to lean against the dresser for support until he put his arm around her and gently led her to the comfortable chair by the window. Then she sat there, shivering as though from fever, while he bathed her head with cologne and rubbed her icy hands. He watched the shadows slip from her eyes as gradually she realized who he was and why he was here.

Although the blood had returned to the pinched whiteness of her face, her voice, when she tried to speak, was stiff as though rusty from disuse.

"How did you know?" she asked.

"I didn't, Señora."

He handed her a cigarette, lighted it for her and sat on the edge of the bed, knowing that she was waiting for him to explain why he had returned, wondering how much he should tell her.

He searched for words to describe his thought processes, how he had shuffled and reshuffled the facts that lay strewn like jigsaw pieces across the surface of his mind without seeing the obvious connection between them. How could he explain to her that a few careless words had caused him, providentially, to rearrange the pieces and save her life when she did not know the shape or size of any of the pieces, or which came first, which second? It would be difficult to reconstruct his reasoning even for the sergeant, who had access to all the facts and who had, through his own chance selection of words, redirected the inspector's thinking and precipitated the solution to the puzzle.

It had happened the way those things so often do, a

flash of illumination when it was least expected. All the way up the stone steps the sergeant had been silent, absorbed in some secret concentration of his own. As they passed through the gate, he pointed to a car that gleamed whitely in the attenuated light.

"Remember the tourist I told you about, the one who was talking to the guide when I arrested him?" he asked. "She was a small woman, blonde, just like the Señora Prewitt. I thought she looked familiar." He went over to examine the car more closely, touched the dolls that hung from the mirror. "There's no doubt about it, she's the one. Imagine giving a fifty-peso tip to someone for recommending a hotel. . . . Why, for that she could have bought something!"

"Bought something!" The inspector repeated the catalytic phrase in astonishment, instantly visualizing every detail. . . . The guide leaning over the white convertible . . . the sergeant waiting in the police car behind it . . . the bag of stones. "Of course she bought something!" he exclaimed.

With the key to the puzzle the rest of the segments automatically interlocked. The whole picture emerged so that he knew why the emerald was not found in the village or on the guide and why the little tourist was in danger.

The woman was looking at him curiously, expectantly. "You must have known, somehow," she insisted stubbornly.

"About the guide? No, I didn't know he was here." It was easier to deny it to her than it was to himself. Something had sparked his immediate alarm when she was not on the terrace or in the lounge. Something had sent him rushing down the walkway to break into the ominous quiet of her room. Sergeant Roberto would label it "instinct." But was not instinct just another form of thought with a logic of its own? Aloud he said, as much to himself as to her, "I told you that nothing is un-related." Then, "I came back to ask you what you bought from the guide."

She stared at him in amazement as though he were some supernormal being, possessed of omniscience. "Some amethysts—but how could you have known I bought anything?"

He ignored the question. "Only some amethysts—are you sure?"

"Why, of course, they're over there on the floor. They're not valuable—I almost threw them away."

There was no mistaking her confusion, yet she must know about the emerald—not its value, perhaps, but that the guide had sold it to her along with the other stones. Certainly no woman would purchase anything without examining it!

As he crossed the room to pick up the stones, suspicion ruffled his sympathy for her. Almost he expected, when he opened the sack, to find the emerald gone; expected her to deny that it had ever been there, but there it lay under the tissue-wrapped amethysts.

"You really didn't look them over," he said.

"No, not carefully. You see, I didn't want to buy them. He almost forced them on me. They're not valuable, are they? I remember now, the guide asked me about them too." Her face twisted with bewilderment. "What is in that sack besides the amethysts?"

The inspector took the jewel out, holding it up between his thumb and forefinger so that it sparkled like a piece of colored glass. "This, Señora, is what the guide was after. To a jeweler it would be an emerald. To Luis Pérez it was a road to wealth. . . . To you it was a road to death. . . . To my wife it's a reward."

He paused, as if there were more, and Jessie, captured by the fanciful pattern of his thinking, asked softly, "And to you, Inspector?"

187

"To me, from the very beginning it has been just one thing—the clue to a murder."

He had come back to sit on the bed's edge again, still staring at the green stone that shimmered in his hand so that he missed her expression when she said, "The Randalls, their murder."

He looked up quickly, mystified. "Señora, how did you know?"

"Maybe in the same way you knew about the guide. I've thought of them so often. They were killed the day I entered Mexico, I traveled the road they took. . . . As you see I held the clue to their murder." She paled suddenly as if with appalled understanding. "Is that why the guide tried to kill me? Did he do it?"

The inspector was taken aback. The idea that the Indians had killed and robbed the tourists was so stubbornly wedged across the opening of his mind that he was not able, immediately, to budge it. Luis, the murderer? He said doubtfully, "I don't know," then admitted reluctantly, "Nothing is impossible." Immediately he found himself assessing the extent of the guide's involvement, weighing possibility against probability, fact against theory.

He sat in rocklike immobility, staring at the emerald as if the answer lay there in one of the glittering green facets; and Jessie's eyes were drawn to it, too, fascinated by its brilliant significance.

"It's unlikely he fired the actual shot," the inspector said at last. "As unlikely as winning the National Lottery —but still he was holding one of the tickets." He nodded speculatively at the jewel.

"You mean he could have planned it," Jessie prompted.

It was the possibility the inspector was groping for and, with uncanny perception, the little señora had synthesized it for him. He was pleased with her and with the

188

idea. It was, perhaps, only necessary to adapt his original theory, not to discard it completely.

"At least that's a definite possibility," he said cautiously. "We can't be certain until we question him. But this is one thing we can be certain of," he continued, holding up the stone. "Our guide knows where he got it —and he'll tell us! You can be sure of that!"

He dropped the gem into his pocket casually as if that ended its value and abruptly changed the subject. "About yourself, Señora. I hope this hasn't spoiled your holiday, that you won't be afraid to stay on in Mexico."

Jessie smiled pensively. "No, I'm not afraid to stay. . . . You know, Inspector, it's only when you don't know why things happen to you that you're really frightened." She paused to study him searchingly, then continued, "Remember, Inspector, tonight on the terrace you said there are always reasons for everything? You've proved your point. I'm leaving Mexico and going home, not because of this, not even because I want to. I must find out the reasons why other things have happened to me."

Although he only vaguely understood what she was talking about, he realized that what she was saying had some personal urgency and felt impelled to warn her. "Señora," he said gently, "we can usually find the reasons for things, but we can't always change them."

"I know, Inspector. And if I can't change them, I'll probably be back."

She spoke more loudly than she usually did and he wondered whether her words were meant for him or the tall, gray-haired man who had stopped outside the doorway to talk with Sergeant Roberto.

A sudden curiosity tugged at him. Why, out of all the thousands of tourists who entered Mexico each year, had fate, in its weaving, selected this particular woman? Obviously the experience had some unusual significance for her and he was reminded again of his own theory that nothing was unrelated, nothing happened by accident.

Later, when he had time, he would discuss it with Sergeant Roberto. Theresa would cook a meal for them on her new stove and they would talk about the case . . . the Randalls . . . the Indians . . . the guide . . . the little *turista*. They would speculate about the lives of all of them and perhaps they would discover the reasons why the threads of their destinies were chosen to entwine.

ON THE FAST new highway between Mexico City and Monterrey a few early trucks were rumbling northward toward the border. Milky mists still lay over the slopes and veiled the distant hills.

The sun had not yet risen, but in the Indian village above the road the women were already firing the kilns. Thinly clad children were huddling close to the primitive ovens gathering warmth against the morning chill or chasing the processions of scrawny brown chickens that paraded everywhere, through the thick yellow grass between the huts, around the refuse pile, along the narrow dirt street.

Like almost everyone else in the village Manuel was awake before dawn. He squatted outside his hut, eating a handful of cooked beans, and watched the activity around the kilns.

Periodically when a truck passed on the highway below, bubbles of memory about the "accident" and the dead *turista* still burst against the surface of his mind, but they were less vivid today than they had been yesterday and his attention was easily held by the lusterless shapes of clay that were ready for baking. Within an hour the heat would magically transform them into shiny brown pots and ash trays to be loaded on the burros for market.

The baking of the pottery always fascinated Manuel so he failed to hear the car climb the access road to the village, and realized that it was there only when the door slammed. He turned to see the guide coming toward him down the narrow street. The guide was not alone. With him was another man, a large man, dark, like the Indians from the northern villages.

A twinge of uneasiness caught at Manuel's throat, starting the bubbles of memory again. . . . The dead *turista* in her flowered dress . . . the glass all over the highway . . . the police coming to look for the ring. Instinctively he hid his face, bending over to pick up a stick and poke at the dirt in front of him with studied concentration, but all the time he was watching them surreptitiously—the huge, dark man with the guide and the guide himself who was strangely disheveled.

Now they stopped to talk together. The guide was looking directly at Manuel and, even before his guilty mind told him that they were talking about him, even before the guide pointed to him, the tiny hairs had stiffened at the back of Manuel's neck. Nervousness washed over him. And as they drew nearer and nearer, his eyes grew darker and wider with apprehension.